MILF CHRONICLES OMNIBUS

SADIE THATCHER

Copyright © 2021 by Sadie Thatcher

All rights reserved.

No part of this book may be reproduced in any form or by any electronic or mechanical means, including information storage and retrieval systems, without written permission from the author, except for the use of brief quotations in a book review.

🕮 Created with Vellum

INTRODUCTION

Welcome to the omnibus edition of the MILF Chronicles Series. This series marks a return to the Bimbo Ward world and the satellite B Clinics.

This book will feature older women becoming bimbo MILFs. There is something different about a bimbo with experience and the bimbos in the MILF Chronicles will definitely have experience. And what experience they still lack, will definitely be made up for.

THANKS FOR THE MAMMARIES

"Welcome, Mrs. Thurman," Dr. Coulson said as he welcomed Shannon Thurman into his office. "Please take a seat."

"Thank you," Shannon said as she did just that, taking a seat in front of his desk as the doctor took his seat behind the desk. "I'm sure I look a bit nervous. I've never done anything like this before."

"You aren't the first woman to get nervous in your situation," Dr. Coulson said with a comforting smile. "I'm sure you'll feel much better afterwards. I understand you are here for the mommy makeover, as we like to call it."

Shannon swallowed hard, steeling herself against her own anxiety. "That's right. The kids are finally out on their own and I've been meaning to rejoin the workforce. After over 20 years as a stay-at-home mom, I'm ready to get back out there. But I figured it wouldn't hurt to make a few improvements first. It's a tough job market and looking a little younger and being a bit more attractive can't hurt, right?"

Shannon was very aware of her increasing age. Her husband, Doug, who was sitting out in the waiting room, had just celebrated his 50th birthday. She was two years behind him, but she could feel it coming at her fast. She knew age was just a number, but it could not hurt to look a little younger, at least during her job interviews. Shannon figured a little botox and filler could be used to tighten up her skin and give her the appearance of being a few years younger, even if it was only temporary.

Of course, the big change Shannon wanted was a breast augmentation. It was not that she was unhappy with the size of her breasts, but she did not like how they had deflated after breastfeeding and then begun to sag over the years. A push-up bra helped keep her bust looking full, but it was annoying having to rely on bras to get the look she wanted. Shannon simply did not want to have to worry about every detail of her appearance anymore. She wanted to have a little work done so she would not have to think about it all the time.

"You are not the first woman to come to that conclusion," the doctor said. "And we here at B Clinic believe we can help you with everything you want and so much more. I believe you will be incredibly happy with the results. When you leave here you will look like a new woman. You can trust me on that."

"I thought this was just a consolation," Shannon said, surprised at how quickly everything was moving. "I wasn't expecting to go through with this now."

"My apologies," Dr. Coulson said. "Somehow I was led to believe you were looking for a quick fix up. But that could be me misunderstanding my secretary. It's all my fault."

Shannon believed the doctor, but having seen the secretary, she doubted the mixup was actually Dr. Coulson's fault. The secretary was a complete bimbo as far as Shannon was concerned. She was honestly surprised the woman could count to 10, let alone manage the office. She looked like she was 20 years old with more tits than brains. The secretary had clearly had a lot of work done and she made for a good advertisement of the clinic's services, but she left something to be desired in the intelligence department.

"It's okay," Shannon said.

"Although, if you go through with the procedure today, I'll cut the fees in half," the doctor offered. "That's quite a deal."

Shannon had already been pricing out her makeover and had come to terms with the high cost. However, she figured it would be worth it in the end, paying for itself once she had secured a job, what with the higher pay she expected to receive. However, a makeover at half the cost was a significant reduction. That was hard to pass up.

"I'd have to bring my husband in for that decision," Shannon said. "We weren't planning this to happen so fast."

"I can have Staci escort him back right away, if you want."

Shannon nodded her head, giving her permission. Dr. Coulson picked up his phone and contacted his secretary, passing her the news. There was a knock at the door a minute later and the incredibly stacked Staci minced into the room on sky-high heels, followed closely behind by Doug.

"Thank you," Dr. Coulson said as Doug took a seat beside his wife. "That will be all, Staci."

Staci smiled inanely as she was dismissed.

"Doug," Shannon said, turning to her husband. "Dr. Coulson has offered half off the makeover if we do it today. That seems like a really good deal, but I wanted to check with you first. I imagine there will be some tough recovery time this week. I won't be as active around the house and might need some help with things."

"Wow, that's a great deal," Doug said. "Honey, you do what you want. You know I'll support you no matter what. If you feel comfortable going through with it today, then I can make it work on my end. I have the money ready to go, so that's not an issue. But I want you to feel comfortable, not only with the procedures, but with yourself."

Shannon had always appreciated Doug's support. Not that there were many husbands who would complain when their wives decided to get a significant cosmetic makeover to look younger and prettier. That seemed like a given.

Actually, there was one area where Doug had been less than supportive of Shannon. It had to do with her going back to work. She had insisted that was her plan all along, from the very beginning of their marriage. She would stay home with the kids while they grew up, but she would return to work when they were out of the house. However, Doug liked the idea of his wife staying at home. He liked the idea of her not working. It made him feel better about himself, knowing he was supporting the woman he loved.

Not that Doug would do anything to stop her from finding a job. He wanted her to be happy. If that meant she went back to work, then he would live with that. However, he definitely wanted her to feel comfortable continuing to stay at home. They were associate members at a country club. He figured they could become full members and she could take up tennis or some other sport if she wanted to stay active and mingle with people. That was his dream for her.

"How about this?" Dr. Coulson offered. "It sounds like your husband is on board, Mrs. Thurman. Let's finish the consultation and then you can decide if you want to proceed today or schedule something for another time, if at all. But the half off deal is only good for today, so please keep that in mind."

"Sounds good to me," Doug said. "Shannon?"

"I think that's smart," Shannon said. "Yes, let's continue with the consolation. I'll let you know what I decide."

Doug got up and returned to the waiting room. Meanwhile, Dr. Coulson continued the consultation, discussing Shannon's desires. Her tastes were simple. She wanted fuller breasts and a younger looking face. Both were things Dr. Coulson assured her he could give her. When it came to the physical examination, Dr. Coulson was both detailed and efficient. Shannon turned pink as she removed her clothing, but she felt better as the examination got underway. Dr. Coulson was completely professional and by the end of the examination, she could almost ignore the fact she was topless.

"You can put your top back on," Dr. Coulson said. As she did so, he continued speaking. "I am completely confident I can give you exactly the look you want. You'll look younger and prettier for sure. And if we do it right, we can have you looking that way for years, not just months."

Shannon had wanted this moment to happen for years. She had been secretly planning this for the past five years. However, now that it was time to actually make the decision, she felt frozen. This was a huge step. But really, there was only one answer she could give. Of course she wanted this. And the sooner the better. With Doug behind her, Shannon gave Dr. Coulson her answer.

"Let's do it today."

"Terrific," Dr. Coulson said, clapping his hands and rubbing them together. "Just give me a moment to get everything ready. In a few minutes we'll have you asleep on the operating table and when you wake up, you'll look better and younger than ever."

Shannon felt overwhelmed by the sudden movement. Before she knew what was happening, Dr. Coulson had brought in nurses to get her prepped for surgery and he had notified Doug of her decision. Before she knew it, she had been stripped down by the nursing staff and placed on the operating table. Moments later she found herself quickly drifting off to sleep as she was asked to count down from 100. She was out before she reached 96.

The doctor was a talented surgeon. He had performed thousands of mommy makeovers in his years in practice with the B Clinic. When he first started, he had been all about keeping it simple, but seeing all the advancements the researchers at Ward B were making, it did not take long for Dr. Coulson to make his own foray into the world of the cutting edge. He had been hesitant to turn his thriving practice into what amounted to a bimbo conversion center, but he had long ago assuaged his discomfort. Of course, it helped having a bimbo like Staci around at the office to keep himself occupied during his downtime. And then there was his wife. He was never unhappy to go home when he had his own bimbo to go home to every night.

However, as much as Dr. Coulson could have radically changed Shannon's body using the techniques and technologies his connection to Ward B had given him, that was not what the client or his patient had asked him for. Had he been asked to turn Shannon into a 20-year-old hottie with a daddy complex, he could have done it without issue. But that was not what was desired in this case. He actually had to restrain himself from going too far. He was so used to making extreme changes to the women who came under his care. In comparison, Shannon was a simple case.

Not that Shannon's makeover was completely what she had been planning for. Yes, her breasts would be fuller, but they would be bigger than she had originally figured for. Her lips and butt would also become bigger and her waist smaller. She was getting the whole package, although a streamlined version of it.

With all the technology at Dr. Coulson's disposal, he could have transformed Shannon's body without a hint of scarring or even artificial implants. That was the power of the tools he had access to use. However, the doctor was a surgeon by training and at heart. He preferred using implants and other artificial means to reshape his patients, giving them an obviously enhanced appearance. To him, that was where real feminine beauty could be found. It was in the artificial, showcasing the extent a woman was willing to go to in her quest to look her best.

Although there was one area where Dr. Coulson happily used the technological marvels he had in his possession. That was recovery. The invasive procedures women chose to undergo to enhance their beauty could take weeks and often months to fully recover from. It was that recovery that scared so many women away, knowing it was more than just the risk of surgery, but the high level of effort required just to go about daily tasks in the weeks that followed the operation.

Luckily, Dr. Coulson could cut the recovery time down to a couple hours with the help of the Ward B research. The only problem was he could not outright advertise such medical marvels without arousing suspicion. It was not something that he talked about, not wanting to draw the ire of the medical board. They would want to review his data, making sure that everything he did was in line with modern medical practice and ethics. Not that his patients ever complained. Then again, with his complete list of services, his patients rarely were in a mood to complain when he had finished with them.

Shannon's surgery took several hours. The breast augmentation was simple enough. Doug had ended up choosing her final size. Had Shannon had her choice, she barely would have been big enough to be worth looking at. After Doug intervened on sizing, Shannon would be the envy of every woman in her neighborhood and the focus of male gazes. Of course, Shannon's breasts were only one part in a much larger package.

With her breasts done, Dr. Coulson moved to Shannon's face. He gave her pouty lips and large expressive eyes. Her cheekbones were perfect, but her nose was just a little too big. He made a slight correction.

Then Dr. Coulson began his work on Shannon's skin. She had wanted her face to appear more youthful, but the doctor saw the need to give her body an all around tightening. Wrinkles disappeared around her eyes and mouth as her skin became taut. This was true everywhere, with her skin smoothing out wrinkles and removing cellulose and other dermal markings.

It was only after Shannon's skin had been repaired that her waist was taken in and her butt expanded. It was a combined operation, with fat getting sucked out of Shannon's belly area and injected into her ass as part of a Brazilian butt lift.

When Dr. Coulson had finished his work, he looked down at Shannon's sleeping form with a broad smile on his face. It was hard to know if Shannon was his best work ever, but it certainly seemed to be up there. He only wished the client, Doug, had been more excited about all the changes he could have made. There was so much more he could have done.

Waking up from the anesthetic, Shannon felt groggy. She found herself in a pink room, sitting in a chair rather than lying down in a bed. This was unexpected. And she almost forgot what she was doing there. Almost.

Shannon looked down to see her breasts pushing out against the hospital smock. She pulled at the collar of the smock to get a better view of her new tits.

"That's, um, really big," Shannon commented to herself. She was at a loss for words. She was sure she had not meant for her breasts to end up this big. Maybe it was just due to swelling. That seemed as good an idea as any. She was completely unaware of Dr. Coulson's recovery techniques. For all the drastic changes that had been made to Shannon's body, she had largely recovered from it all. It would have been a great topic for a paper, but that would only serve to draw additional attention to himself. Dr. Coulson did not need nor want the publicity.

"Oh good, you're awake," Dr. Coulson said as he walked into Shannon's recovery room. She noticed he did not knock. He just barged in like he owned the place. Then again, he probably did.

"Something seems wrong," Shannon said, although she still could not put a finger on what exactly was wrong.

"It can certainly feel that way when you first wake up from anesthesia. I've seen some patients panic and try to climb out of their chair and nearly hurt themselves. That's why you're restrained. It's for you safety."

Shannon looked down and pulled at his wrists and ankles. She had been completely restrained. Neither her legs, nor her arms, were capable of movement beyond the slight give in the leather straps.

"What's going on?" she asked, her voice quaking with fear. Her concern over her physical condition had been replaced with the heaving strapping which kept her confined not to a bed, but to a reclining chair.

"It's time for the second part of your makeover," Dr. Coulson said with a knowing smirk. "It wouldn't do to send you out into the world with the same mind as you had before. I have upgraded your body and you deserve an upgraded mind as well."

"What?" Shannon nearly screamed. She looked around the room, frantically searching out a means of escape. Then her eyes fell to her chest. Her breasts were large, far larger than she had asked for. She wanted fuller, but these were simply huge to her. "This isn't what I asked for. What kind of operation are you running here? I demand to talk to my husband."

"You want Doug to comfort you?" Dr. Coulson asked. "I can have him come in. Last I heard one of the nurses was giving him a massage while he waited for your procedure to be done."

"You mean he agreed to all of this?" Shannon asked, a sense of betrayal welling up inside of her. This was not how the day was supposed to go. She was not supposed to wake up with tits looking like they fit on a bimbo. And it was not supposed to be Doug pulling the strings from behind the scenes.

"I merely gave him some options," Dr. Coulson answered. "He only wants what's best for you. As do I. We want you to be happy and neither of us believe you will be happy by returning to the workforce. But luckily, we have options to make that a certainty. By the time you leave here, you will have no interest in working ever again."

"But..." Shannon said, but she could not think of the words to describe how she felt. She felt betrayed and scared, but at the same time, she felt really good. She felt younger, at least physically. The aches and pains that came with middle age were gone. And to be honest, she was a little horny. Her arousal had jumped, giving her a new baseline that would make it much easier to get into the mood. Doug would, of course, be appreciative of that.

"Don't worry your pretty little head about a thing," Dr. Coulson said. Even though Shannon was still fully herself mentally, he could not help but view her as the final product. She was a bimbo. That was her destiny, even if she did not yet realize that fact.

"What are you going to do to me?" Shannon asked. She

still sounded scared, but more and more, she was growing curious about this whole process. Clearly she had not read the fine print on the documents she signed.

"The details are hugely complicated, but the general idea is I will be replacing some of your memory engrams," Dr. Coulson answered. "I will be deleting some memories, altering others, and giving you completely new ones as well. We are, after all, a product of our experiences. As much as nature gives us the basic building blocks, it is how we nurture those building blocks that ultimately decides who we are. And for you, I believe we will be giving you a much happier and fulfilling life. You will love the new you. Then again, you won't be able to avoid loving the new you. It will be all you know."

Shannon swallowed hard, trying to steel herself for what would happen next. She knew she had no choice. She was fully restrained and unable to call for help. She doubted anyone would come to her aid if she screamed. More than likely the room had been sound proofed. The nurses, the secretary, and even her husband would not come to help her. She was in this alone and unable to change her situation. Her only hope was to go along with it.

"Can you do me a favor?" Shannon asked. If she had no choice in going through with the memory alterations, she might as well get something positive out of it.

"I can certainly try," Dr. Coulson said as he turned on the computer monitor connected to the chair Shannon was strapped to.

"There was an incident in college," Shannon said. "A man. He, um, did something to me. I'd rather not remember it."

Dr. Coulson nodded his head. Despite his profession and specialty, Dr. Coulson had always believed there was a special place in hell for people who traumatized others. He did not know the details of Shannon's pain, but he had several ways to deal with the problem without further details. The more traumatic an event, the more the memory engrams stood out. It would be easy to find and remove. Although it would be even easier to simply build Shannon a new backstory, one that would preclude her from being in the negative situation to begin with.

It truly was amazing what Dr. Coulson could achieve, as could all the doctors affiliated with Ward B. The chain of B Clinics were all different, but they all had access to the same techniques and technology. The medical achievements that had been made would shock the world. However, the greater shock would come from how those techniques and technologies had been developed and how they were first used. It was the stigma that created that meant they would take much longer to reach the mainstream of the medical community. It really was a matter of the prudes and those who were perpetually offended that prevented these great breakthroughs from being utilized outside the bimbofication field.

"I can do that," Dr. Coulson said. He had taken the Hippocratic oath when he became a doctor. Yes, there were some fizzy lines in his field, but the fact all his patients came away happier and often healthier gave him comfort and allowed him to navigate the ethical and moral gray zone in which he worked. At the very least, he could always answer to an inquiry with the fact that he always did what was best for the future of his patients, even if it meant sacrificing the present and the past.

"Whenever you're ready, Doc," Shannon said. She had given up on fighting. There was no point. Her only thought was that she might as well do all she could to improve herself. As much as she got far more than she bargained for with her body, from what she could tell strapped down into a chair, she looked great. That had to count for something.

"Very well," Dr. Coulson said as he started to attach wired

electrodes to the sides of Shannon's head. He then dropped a pair of goggles onto her face, covering her eyes. Then he plugged noise cancelling earbuds into her ears to completely cut her off from the outside world. He had complete control of her visual and auditory stimuli. Coupled with the electrodes on her head, he could ultimately identify the memory engrams that needed altering as well as create entirely new ones.

"Should I say goodbye?" Shannon asked, wondering if when the procedure was over she would still be herself.

"You'll still be you," Dr. Coulson answered. "You'll just be a better version of you. Trust me. You'll be all smiles when we're done here. You'll be recommending my services to everyone you know very soon."

Shannon nodded her head. Not that she could see anything. The goggles were blacked out, the lenses actually small screens to feed her mind new information. The system was completely immersive.

Dr. Coulson began running the memory engram program. He had originally planned to just make a few small alterations, giving her the chance to retain who she was, but with a sexier outcome. However, her request to remove a traumatic memory from her college career gave the doctor a different idea about how to achieve his goals. It would take more time, but he was sure her husband would not mind. He was well taken care of.

Taking a sip of coffee, Dr. Coulson watched the monitor carefully as Shannon's brain was mapped, specifically her memories. He only wished he could actually see the memories play out on the monitor, but the technology was not that advanced yet. Maybe someday, assuming he did not retire early to spend more time with the bimbos he had at home. That was common among the Ward B and B Clinic doctors. They were paid well and they often retired early. It was considered a perk of the job, especially as they often got to keep the strays that came their way.

With the goal for Shannon to be roughly eight years younger than she really was, having just hit 40, instead of her real age of 48, Dr. Coulson decided to go back to her college days and make a few alterations. In many ways, they were simple alterations, but they would help cut out the years needed to properly drop Shannon's age. It would also make it easy to remove her traumatic memory from college.

Shannon's new backstory was simple. She made it into college, barely. She joined the cheerleaders and got involved in sorority life immediately. That was when she met Doug. She was a freshman and he was a grad student. They fell in love. However, the pressures of her classes, her cheer schedule, and her sorority responsibilities were too much. She failed out of college in her first semester. Not to mention she got pregnant early on. Shannon went from a solid major with career prospects to a college dropout with a baby on the way.

Once those early memory engrams were added, it was easy to go through and make simple edits to the rest of her memories. Shannon had become far more interested in her appearance. She also more readily adopted an attitude that she was not college or work material. Her place was in the home, first taking care of the kids and now that they were grown and fully out of the house, taking care of her husband. It was those actions, like cooking dinner or giving him a welcome home from work blowjob that gave her life meaning. And now she could view her mommy makeover as not just wanting to look her best, but as a reward for her husband for being such a good man to her, for providing for her all these years, for being the love of her life.

Much of the computer processes were automated. As much as Dr. Coulson was well-experienced using the memory engram manipulator, it felt like a plug and play system. He only had to tell the computer his intentions and it would find a way to make it happen. Over time, the doctor had learned a few tricks here or there, but the interface was as intuitive as could be. The program was clearly designed for non-technical people, which Dr. Coulson appreciated. If it were more difficult, he still would have been able to use it, but the simple interface meant he could sometimes work with a few distractions. Those distractions often came from one of the nurses or Staci dropping in to suck his cock while he worked.

However, with Shannon, Dr. Coulson had no such distractions. It was just him and Shannon, working together to bring about greater harmony. Not that Shannon needed to do much other than sit there under the spell of the computer that was essentially rewriting her brain.

When it was all said and done, Shannon was a completely different person.

"Hi, Doc," Shannon said cheerily as he pulled the goggles off her head.

"How are you feeling, Shannon?" Dr. Coulson asked.

The first few minutes after memory engram integration had completed was always the hardest on the patient. Sometimes there were lingering feelings from erased or altered memories that left the patient confused and emotional. No technology was perfect, especially when dealing with the human brain.

"I feel great," she chirped. "And look, you gave me great big titties. I love 'em."

Already he could see the massive change in Shannon's demeanor. And she seemed far more simple than she did before. The whole package was quite impressive. Shannon was very much a bimbo now and she did not seem to be experiencing any adverse side effects. As far as she was concerned, she had always been like this, minus the plastic surgery, of course. That was new, but that was also what she wanted.

"I'm glad to hear it," Dr. Coulson said with a smile. "Another satisfied patient. Let me get you unhooked and then we can get you changed so you can meet up with your husband."

At the mention of Doug, Shannon grew starry eyed. She really did love him. And unlike before, when her love bond had been strong enough to at least mostly withstand the betrayal she had felt before, now it was even stronger. It was not just love, but lust that bonded her to her husband. She had developed a submissiveness toward him that gave her life greater definition.

Not that Shannon realized this, of course. To her, nothing had changed. She did not remember a time in the past 20 years when she was not a bimbo. This was who she was. And other than a few mental tricks she would have to perform to maintain the fact she was legally 48 years old, but mentally 40, she was ready to return to her life as she now remembered it, even if it was a bit different from the life she had actually lived thus far. The fact her math skills might have degraded a bit to make the mental trick work was rarely viewed as a problem. In fact, it was often viewed as a feature.

Dr. Coulson released the straps restraining Shannon to the chair. She flexed her arms and legs with her newfound freedom and smiled.

"Thank you, Doc," Shannon said as she pushed herself to her feet. She was a little unsteady at first, what with her new proportions. And her muscle memory would take some retraining. That was not so easily changed via the memory engram procedure. But it would only take. Few days, or weeks at most, for Shannon to feel completely at home with her new self.

"You're welcome," Dr. Coulson said, smiling. He always loved this part. Yes, it was disheartening sometimes to see women before they had embraced their bimboness, but once they had gone bimbo, they were all smiles and so was the doctor. It was moments like these when he really loved his work. He not only made women more beautiful, at least in his eyes, but he made them happier as well. A single day in his clinic was like getting cosmetic surgery, spending the day at a relaxing skin spa, and spending a lifetime of weekly appointments with a therapist all in one. There was no comparison.

Shannon bounced over to a full length mirror on the wall. It had been placed there for just the purpose Shannon now used it for: primping and making sure she looked her best. After all, that was now forefront in her thoughts. She knew she was a bimbo. She knew her value was in her submissiveness to her husband and in her body. Her brain mostly just made sure everything worked right. Her thoughts were just noise that got in the way, making it easy for her to ignore them.

"Such a MILF," Shannon said as she squeezed her tits through the medical smock she still wore. "But now that I've got big tits, I need to do something about this hair. I think I'm gonna go blonde." Shannon started giggling at the thought of her with blonde hair.

Dr. Coulson could only chuckle as she made her self-appraisal. He had offered to change her hair color, but Doug had pushed the idea aside. There were some things he wanted her to work for. He supposed Doug liked the idea of dark roots on his bimbo wife to be. And in a way, the doctor agreed with him. Yes, the upkeep was higher, requiring regular salon appointments, but she would be going to those anyway with her newfound vanity. And the coloring process from brown to blonde did allow for more variation in styles.

"I'm sure your husband will love that," Dr. Coulson said. "Now let's get you dressed so you can go see him. He's waiting for you."

"Oh goodie," Shannon squealed as she bounced up onto her toes, causing her tits to bounce and bound on her chest. That, in turn, set her to giggling, as she found that she loved making her tits bounce. Even with them covered as much as they were, she loved watching them in the mirror. However, the chance to put real clothes on, clothes that would highlight her body and show off her new assets was too important to get caught up in watching her tits. That could come later.

Dr. Coulson opened a small cabinet next to the mirror. Inside was an outfit for Shannon to wear, as well as a pair of high heels. He had not gone to the same lengths as he had with other women before her to force Shannon to wear high heels. Again, that offer was turned down by Doug, as he wanted her to still be able to play tennis at the country club, even if it had not been a common activity for her before. And playing tennis with any amount of skill required being able to move across the court with some degree of speed and that just was not possible if she was forced to mince around on the court in high heels.

The outfit that had been chosen for Shannon was relatively simple. It was a red wrap dress with a plunging neckline to make sure she had a deep valley of cleavage on display. It hugged her waist tightly before it flared out around her hips. The dress was short compared to what Shannon previously would have considered appropriate, but it was not so short that she risked flashing the matching red thong that had been provided for her. The red and black heels completed the outfit. There was no provided bra, but the truth was, with her new tits, she did not really need a bra. They stood out on her chest just fine without one. Although she would definitely need a heavy duty bra to play tennis, that would be obtained in good time.

Once she had changed, Dr. Coulson led her out toward the waiting area where she could be reunited with her husband.

"Doug," she squealed as soon as she saw him. She minced over in her high heels and wrapped him up in a big hug, pressing her new big tits against his chest and giving him a passionate kiss on the lips.

Doug responded to his remade wife instantly, both in returning her embrace and kiss, but also in getting hard. His cock strained at just the sight of her, but feeling her body press up against his own was more than enough to get him ready.

"Welcome to your new life, Mrs. Thurman," Staci said. "Your husband processed all of the remaining paperwork while you were in the back. You're both free to go."

"It was an honor working with you," Dr. Coulson said. "And tell your friends. I get most of my clients by referral."

"Oh, I will, Doc," Shannon said after she and Doug broke their kiss. Although his hands had drifted down her back and found her ass. He was squeezing her cheeks, making her even wetter. She had never been this horny before.

"Let's go, sweetie," Doug said as he let go of his wife and gave her a little swat on the ass to get her moving toward the door.

Shannon cooed at the attention she received and then minced toward the door. Her husband had given her an order and she was not someone who could disobey an order from her husband. As his wife, it was unthinkable.

The ride home was pure torture for Shannon. She could see Doug's cock tenting his pants, but there was nothing she could do for him while they drove. Yes, she had offered to blow him, but he had refused, wanting instead to save himself for when they got home. She could not argue with that.

However, Shannon had become acutely aware of Doug's presence. She had never realized how good he smelled before. Stuck in the small confines of their car, she was even more aware of it. And just the smell of him was enough to turn her on. Her thong was already wet.

And the moment they were home, Shannon wanted to drag her husband into the house so he could ravish her. However, there was no way she could do that. Her submissiveness had been turned up to such a degree that she could not lead him into the house like that. Not that Doug was avoiding their future coupling. He just had more patience than his now bimbofied wife did.

"Come here," Doug finally said when they were safely inside. He grabbed Shannon by the shoulders and pulled her in close. She melted against him, loving how hot he felt against her. She could feel his cock through his pants. She had no idea how he had managed to avoid ripping her clothes off right there and then, or even before then. But there was a reason Doug was the man of the house. Shannon was not capable of such self control. She would be completely lost, a complete slut, if it were not for him. He had taken her and trained her to be the perfect bimbo wife for him. It was all there in her memories.

Doug guided Shannon toward the bedroom. Once there, he sat down on the bed, leaving Shannon standing there, swaying slightly, always trying to best show off her body. Now that she finally had gotten her big tits, she was more than happy to show them off.

"Do a little dance while you strip for me," Doug said as he pulled out his phone and turned on some music.

Shannon's hips started to move to the beat without her even having to think about it. Then her hands went to her dress as she slowly started to untie it. She took her time, putting on the best show she was able. She might not have had patience for herself, but when Doug gave her an order, she followed it without question.

She did a little turn, making sure to take a moment and shake her ass in Doug's direction. Then she turned quickly and opened the front of her dress, revealing her bare tits in all their glory. Her body was fit and trim beneath her protruding tits. Her little red thong fit snugly against her pussy. Her body hair was gone, erased permanently from her skin. She shucked off the dress, letting it fall down off her shoulders. Shannon swung it around her head once it was free and let it fly toward a chair in the corner.

"How do you like your bimbo?" Shannon asked before she bit her lower lip. She ran her hands down her body, toward her hips. She pulled at the band of her thong. "Should I take it off?"

Doug simply nodded his head. Nothing more needed to be said.

Shannon followed his direction, turning around and then slowly pulling her thong down over her ass. Her pussy came into view, pink and swollen and very wet. She gave her ass a smack and then let the thong fall around her ankles. Shannon turned as she stepped out of her panties, now only wearing her high heels. She stuck a finger into the corner of her mouth, looking both cute and air headed. It was hard to imagine that this woman had been a college graduate just a few hours earlier. Now she looked like a dumb and horny MILF. Then again, that was exactly what she now was.

"Come here," Doug said, beckoning his wife forward.

She stepped toward him and as soon as she was within arm's reach, he grabbed her and sat her down on his lap. "You should call me Daddy now," he whispered into her ear.

"Ooh, yes, Daddy," Shannon cooed.

"Good."

In one smooth motion, Doug flipped Shannon over and stood up, leaving her on her hands and knees on the bed, her ass pointed toward him. It took only a few moments for him to disrobe. His cock was long and hard. He had never been this hard for his wife before, but his wife had never been a bimbo before, even if she remembered otherwise.

Shannon's eyes went wide as he entered her from behind. His cock pressed into her waiting pussy with ease, sliding deep inside of her on his first thrust. And that initial thrust was almost enough to make the horny bimbo that was now Shannon cum. But what was more, she felt as if she was serving her purpose. She had never felt so fulfilled as she was filled with his cock. Shannon, better than ever, now understood her purpose in life. This was where she was meant to be. This was who she was meant to be. Every part of her life was lining up to perfection.

And all the while, Doug fucked his wife from behind, thrusting in and out of her, treating her like she was just there for his own pleasure. Yet, given the changes in Shannon's body and mind, all the things that gave Doug pleasure now gave her pleasure too.

"Harder," Shannon called out as she found herself stuck on the precipice. Her body was poised to cum. The orgasm seemed within reach. But she was not cumming. "Please, fuck me harder, Daddy."

It was the closest Shannon could come to giving her husband an order. But hearing her use his new nickname, he could not stop himself from doing just that. His pace and force increased as he neared his own climax.

Shannon felt a sudden twitch inside her. It was not her body, but Doug's cock that had made the movement, even while he was in the middle of thrusting into her. She knew that twitch well, even from before she was a bimbo. It was his cock's way of telling the both of them that he had passed his point of no return. He was going to cum. The only question was when and where.

"I'm gonna cum," Doug practically roared.

"Do it, Daddy. Cum in my pussy. Fill me up."

And Doug did exactly that. His orgasm was the breaching of a dam. Suddenly his cock was shooting loads of fresh hot seed into Shannon's pussy. She came with him, that flood of cum setting off her own orgasm. It was as if that flood had turned into a torrential river spreading orgasmic pleasure through her body. Her vision turned white as her arms gave way beneath her, her face planting into the bedcovers.

"Oh yes," Shannon called out as her body convulsed with orgasmic ecstasy. Sex had never felt this good before. If there was one thing she was certain of, it was that she was addicted to this. She was addicted to the sexual pleasure that her husband's cock gave her. And she knew they were just getting started. She had big tits to fuck, as well as two more holes. She could keep going for as long as Doug could.

However, Doug needed time to recover. He was not as young as he once was. His virility was never in question, but he made sure he had a few blue pills on hand to make sure his cock was ready to go again before the night was through. In the meantime, Shannon was ushered off to the kitchen to start making dinner. She kept her heels on, but simply put on an apron for cooking. Doug enjoyed watching her work as he sat at the kitchen table.

Later that night they would begin another round of sexual fun, a common occurrence for them now. Sex was a near constant in their lives together. From that day forward, it was a rare day when they did not get each other off in one way or another. But there was still much to be done. Shannon needed a new wardrobe. Doug had taken the time to throw out her ill-fitting and boring clothes. As a bimbo,

Shannon had specific tastes, even if she kept things on the classy side. For she was a well-trained bimbo slut. But she needed new bras anyway, especially so she could complete her tennis outfits. Her big tits needed to be kept in check while she played. Otherwise she might hurt herself.

Doug was thankful everyday for what Dr. Coulson had provided him, even if it had not been something he had initially planned for. It was pure luck that Shannon happened to have chosen a doctor with the B Clinic franchise. But he was not about to take the gift that was now his wife for granted. And between the two of them, they would push their friends and neighbors hard about the benefits that Dr. Coulson could provide, both physical and mental.

As a newly minted bimbo without any grasp of her real past, Shannon was thankful for her tits, her big mammaries. Doug, on the other hand, while enjoying his wife's new body, much preferred the new memories she received, the memories that changed her from a normal middle-aged mother and wife into a hot bimbo MILF. And she was a mother that he definitely enjoyed fucking each and every night. Shannon enjoyed that part too. After all, she was a horny bimbo now and that was what she lived for.

A NEW BEGINNING

Katherine sat at the conference table. There was a pen in her hand and the initial divorce documents were in front of her. She could not believe it had come to this. Her marriage with Mitchell was about to be over.

If Katherine was honest with herself, this day had been coming for years. The only reason she and Mitchell had stayed together was for their kids. But the kids were grown and out of the house. It was just them and it seemed they could no longer pretend to be a loving couple anymore. That was what it had been. It had all been pretend. Sure, they slept in the same bed, but Katherine could not even remember the last time they were intimate together.

"There are two stages to this divorce settlement," her lawyer explained. "There is a pre-settlement award and a post-settlement award. You don't need to sign the whole thing yet. I know how hard this can be. Signing the pre-settlement portion will get the ball rolling, but it doesn't commit you to anything yet, just in case you have second thoughts."

Katherine nodded her head. She could not believe it had come to this. Back in the beginning, she and Mitchell had been very much in love. They could not get enough of each other. But as the years dragged on, when middle age started to settle in, they grew apart. It happened to many couples. They went from classic newly weds to roommates in the span of 20 or so years.

"What is the pre-settlement?" Katherine asked. She had never heard that term before.

"It's something we like to add into our divorce settlements," the lawyer explained. "Many of the women we represent feel the need for a little boost as they re-enter the wider world after years spent in marriage. Think of it as a mommy makeover in your case."

Katherine did not argue with the idea she could use a makeover. She had always been cute, but she felt that way less and less. The stress of the divorce made it all worse. Already short, Katherine had grown more and more pear shaped over the years, her hips dominating her figure. Even her hair looked less than it could have, the stringy brown hair was hard to manage and style.

At least Katherine would not have to worry about money. That was the one benefit of having married Mitchell in the first place. He made better than good money. Her cut of the assets, plus alimony, would mean she would not need to get a job, at least for a long time. Not that she would be able to keep her current lifestyle in its entirety. She would need to downsize her home. She assumed Mitchell would keep the house. He would still have the ability to afford it. And Katherine did not need all that space. A two-bedroom bungalow was all she really needed.

"That sounds nice," Katherine said. "I suppose I could use a bit of a makeover. Maybe they'll teach me what's fashionable these days. I feel like I'm 20 years out of date."

"Yes, well if you just sign on the dotted line," the lawyer said, "we can start getting the pre-settlement processed and send you off to the B Clinic for your makeover."

"Already?" Katherine asked. "You made an appointment for me?"

"We've found it's best to get started on the pre-settlement portion of the divorce right away," the lawyer explained. "It makes the rest of the proceedings much easier to deal with. Trust me."

Katherine nodded her head. She did trust the lawyer. Actually, the whole situation had been an interesting one. Her lawyer had been a friend for many years. She did not even remember how they originally met. But more importantly, Mitchell had been too slow on the uptake to realize what was happening. She had lawyered up first. Mitchell was left to play catchup.

"That makes sense, I think," Katherine said.

"Terrific. Here's the address. They are expecting you this afternoon for your consultation."

The lawyer pushed a card across the table. It was a business card for a Dr. Coulson. It included a phone number and address for B Clinic, whatever that was. There was a handwritten time listed. She would barely have time to get lunch before she needed to report.

"I better be going then," Katherine said as she quickly scrawled a signature on the pre-settlement award documentation. She would need to sign the rest later. She had an appointment to get to.

Rushing out, Katherine forgot the business card. She hurried back to grab it. She did not want to be late.

As soon as she was back in her car, she plugged the address into her phone to get directions. There was a coffee shop near the clinic. That would make for the small lunch she needed to get her through until dinner.

"Hi, I'm Staci," said the receptionist at the front desk as Katherine walked into B Clinic. "How can I help you today?"

Katherine looked up at the large-breasted blonde woman and nearly choked. She had never seen a woman who looked more like a bimbo before. Not that Katherine minded bimbos. She was all for women being whatever they wanted to be. It was an individual choice. Nonetheless, Katherine could not help but feel that women who chose to turn themselves into sexual objects for men, much as Staci seemed to have done, were betraying the hard work of the women who fought for their rights and freedoms.

"My name is Katherine and I have an appointment that my divorce lawyer set up for me."

"Ooh, yeah, I have your name, like, right here and stuff. I'll tell Dr. Coulson you're here."

Katherine watched as Staci pecked out a short sentence on her keyboard. It was a wonder she could type at all, given her long nails. And it was almost comical the way that she had to sit so far back from the computer, just so she could see the keyboard over her prodigious breasts. They were clearly fake, but then again, some women liked that.

There had been a time when Katherine had wondered if she should get implants. Those thoughts had occurred shortly after she noticed how she and Mitchell had started to drift apart. She wondered if bigger breasts would increase his interest in her. However, in the end, she had shut that idea down. Why should she undergo potentially dangerous surgery just to make her husband more sexually attracted to her? It went against her feminist ideals. He should love her for who she was and not expect her to play some fantasy for him.

It was only a moment later that a man in a white lab coat appeared in the reception area.

"Katherine, I presume?" the man said, approaching Katherine and holding out his hand. "I'm Dr. Coulson. I understand your lawyer sent you."

"Yes, that's right," Katherine said as she responded with her own hand, noting that the doctor had a firm handshake. She had always found that attractive in a man. It might have been what first caught her attention of Mitchell. There had been a coed intramural basketball tournament. They had played on opposite teams, she a freshman and he a senior. The game had not been memorable, but the high fives and handshakes after the game were, at least the handshake with Mitchell. He had asked her out a week later and she had accepted. They had been together ever since.

"Let's go back to my office and we can discuss what kind of makeover you're interested in," Dr. Coulson said.

"Sure."

Katherine followed the doctor into the back. Little did she realize that Mitchell was also present. He was waiting in an adjacent room, letting everything play out as it had been planned. Unbeknownst to Katherine, her lawyer was actually good friends with Mitchell. He had been tipped off as soon as she started talking about divorce and a plan had been put into place.

Mitchell had only heard about B Clinic through a friend at work. Doug had raved about what the clinic could do after his wife had made a visit. Mitchell had remembered how Doug would complain about his wife wanting to go back to work. But he had arranged for a mommy makeover for her and she stopped having thoughts about returning to the workforce. Instead, they had increased their membership at the country club and Shannon, his wife, was playing tennis at the club at least three days per week. She might not have been very good, but she enjoyed it and the men at the club enjoyed watching her play. They could not get enough of her in her skimpy tennis outfits, watching the way her tits bounced or her skirts swished up to reveal her thong panties.

For months, Mitchell had been trying to figure out how to arrange for Katherine to visit B Clinic for a makeover. Their relationship had been less than good in recent years. He still loved her, but he had a hard time showing his affection toward her. But when he found out she was going to file for divorce, it was easy enough to add a makeover into the settlement agreement. However, once she had finished at B Clinic, she would not want to get divorced anymore. It would be quite the opposite, in fact. But that was putting the cart before the horse. For now, all he could do was wait.

"Have you thought much about what you would like to have done?" Dr. Coulson asked as he sat down behind his desk. Katherine took a seat opposite him.

"I only just found out about this place about an hour ago," Katherine answered. "I wasn't aware this was an option and I don't actually know what services you provide. My lawyer mentioned a mommy makeover, but even that is just a generic term. It could mean anything from a basic makeup makeover or something more invasive."

It was clear that invasive meant breast implants. She already had an idea that B Clinic was a plastic surgery clinic and not just a fancy salon. Dr. Coulson did not seem like the sort of person who would be styling her hair.

"Let's just say that the sky is the limit here," Dr. Coulson said. "If you could do anything for your appearance, regardless of how odd it might be, what would you do?"

Katherine stopped and thought about her answer. She had not been expecting this line of questioning. It did not help that she felt the stress of the divorce weighing on her. She had not signed the papers yet, but she assumed that would come soon. It was time to say goodbye to the past and to embrace her future, even if that meant she would spend her time going forward alone.

"In a perfect world," Katherine finally began to explain, "my hair would be better and my hips wouldn't dominate my figure so much. And maybe I'd be a bit taller. I get tired of having to always use step stools to reach the top shelves in the kitchen."

Dr. Coulson nodded his head in understanding. He had a keen eye for beautiful women. Katherine had potential, but she was held back by the three things she mentioned. Short was not bad, but he could understand why she wanted to be taller. Adding height would also make her hips seem less wide. It was all a matter of perspective. Yes, when she was so short, her wide hips were a more dominant feature. But add a few inches to her height and she would look decidedly less like a pear.

"What if I told you all those things were fixable?" the doctor asked.

"I'd call bullshit," Katherine answered. "I'd say you were bullshitting me."

"Not at all," Dr. Coulson said. "I don't make offers I can't back up. In fact, not only can I do those things, but I can make you look and feel like a younger woman. And remember, your soon to be ex-husband is paying for all of this as part of the divorce proceedings."

Katherine nodded her head. Yes, that was true. Mitchell was paying for this. And he could afford it too. It was the perfect way to start over. She would look younger and prettier. She might even be able to snag a new man, a man who would treat her the way she deserved.

"I want it all," Katherine finally said.

It took 20 minutes to go through all the options. Once the

floodgates had been opened, Katherine seemed interested in much of what B Clinic had to offer. Not that she wanted the same things that Mitchell wanted. Yes, bigger breasts would be nice, but not overly large. She just wanted to go up a cup size or two. Same for her height. She liked the idea of being taller, but she only wanted to add a couple inches. Basically, she wanted to change everything, but nothing would get taken to the extreme.

"This all looks good," Dr. Coulson eventually said. "And if you have the time, we can get it all done today."

Katherine's eyes bugged out at the sudden offer. She had assumed this would take time to set up. There was paperwork to sign, drugs to procure, not to mention obtaining the implants. It seemed impossible for her consultation to turn into a full blown makeover all at once.

"Don't you think I should wait to think all this over?" Katherine said, suddenly nervous.

"You seem perfectly rational and composed to me," Dr. Coulson answered. "You can wait if you want, but the longer you do, the more likely we'll be booked. Your lawyer begged me to create this opening for you. It's already a two-month wait otherwise. This is a popular makeover season."

Katherine knew the doctor was putting a hard sell on her. If she did not go through with it now, it could be months. And if her divorce was contingent on her completing the pre-settlement, then it would mean delaying the divorce and that was not something she wanted to do.

"Okay, fine, let's do it today."

"Terrific," Dr. Coulson said, rubbing his hands together in satisfaction. "You won't regret this."

Before Dr. Coulson led Katherine into the operating room to begin, he took a short moment to delete her modifications plan. They would not be needing it. Her husband had already completed one and it was his that they would be using. Katherine did not need to know that. She would find out eventually, but by then, it would be too late. And the truth was, he knew she would be much happier after all this was done. She would be a whole new woman and her marriage would be saved.

Katherine's eyes fluttered open many hours later. She felt groggy and achy. Her body felt strange to her, even as she was lying in the darkened recovery room. She had a vague feeling that something was wrong, but she had a hard time identifying what it could be. She remembered agreeing to the makeover. She remembered agreeing to some significant body modifications. Each modification alone might have been normal enough, but combined together, they were massive.

Except as Katherine became more and more aware of her body, she began to realize what the problem was. The doctor had gone to much more extreme lengths than she had thought he would. She raised her head slightly to find two mounds sticking up off her chest. She had only wanted to go a little bigger, but they looked huge. It was hard to tell in the darkened room, but there was no way she would be able to buy bras at the department store anymore with these puppies on her chest. She would need to go the special order route, probably.

Yet, as frustrating as seeing bigger breasts than she had asked for was, she found it difficult to be mad about it. She was sure she would have a few choice words for Dr. Coulson when he came to check on her, but she was not as mad as she had expected. There was a part of her that actually liked them, knowing they would balance out her figure. If anything, she might even be a little top-heavy for once and that gave Katherine a small thrill.

The only question was what else the doctor had done to her without following the plan they had developed together. She had no idea that Mitchell was behind her new body. Not that she was fully aware just how much her body had been changed. She would be almost unrecognizable now.

"Good morning," Dr. Coulson said as he swept into the recovery room. He pulled up the shade on the window, letting in the light from the morning sun.

Katherine blinked rapidly, trying to adjust her vision to the sudden influx of natural light. Once Dr. Coulson started to come back into focus, she realized he had moved to her bedside and was looking down at her with keen interest.

"What did you do to me?" she croaked, her mouth and throat parched from thirst.

"Let me get you a glass of water first," Dr. Coulson answered. "Then while you're drinking, I'll explain everything."

A short moment later the doctor stood beside her once again, holding a cup of water with a plastic straw so that she could drink from her reclined position. She sucked on the straw happily, not noticing how her lips were more plump or the way she puckered them when she drank from the straw.

"I thought about withholding all of this from you until after your makeover is complete, but you won't really be able to understand once I replace your memory engrams. You see, your lawyer isn't really working for you. You chose poorly, not realizing that your lawyer went to high school with your husband. They were good friends growing up. Or at least that is my understanding of their relationship."

Katherine let her jaw drop in surprise. Admittedly, that did little to change her already vacant expression. Her natural expression was one of surprise. When all was said and done, that expression would be completely true. After seeing what a bimbo Doug's wife had turned into, Mitchell wanted the same thing for Katherine. He wanted to have a dumb little housewife to come home to every day. That was her future, whether she wanted it to be or not.

"It's not uncommon for women to be tricked into coming here," Dr. Coulson explained. "I long ago gave up the pretense of caring how women found their way into my hands. What matters is that they are always happy when they leave."

"You're a monster," Katherine said. Her now lubricated throat made it much easier to speak. But that ease also came with the realization that her voice sounded different. It was softer and had a higher pitch.

Dr. Coulson shrugged his shoulders. "I've been called worse. And it's probably true. But that doesn't mean that I don't do good work. The world is a fucked up place. There are monsters who kill and maim. I just make people happy. Sure they might not have the same skill sets as they did when they came in, but they always leave more loving and excited. And to be honest, this world needs more people to love each other. I'm not saying all women should be turned into bimbos, but every bimbo I've created has been a net positive on the world, in my opinion."

It all started to make sense. Katherine realized she should have been more wary when she met Staci. She was every bit the bimbo that Dr. Coulson reveled in. She was clearly a product of his work. Katherine hated the idea of being like her, simple minded and unable to do anything significant without a man's help. She was supposed to be divorcing Mitchell, not turning into his bimbo.

"Do I have a choice?" Katherine asked.

Again, Dr. Coulson shrugged. "I guess that depends on what you think your options are. The truth is, if I leave you as you are now, you'll go mad with lust in a matter of weeks. Your body has been significantly altered. You might not notice it now, with the drugs that are still flowing through your system, but your baseline arousal has jumped precipitously. I'd give it a week before you picked up a guy at a bar for a one night stand. By three weeks, you wouldn't be able to control yourself. Your body has needs now. An unfocused mind will crack under the pressure."

Katherine swallowed hard. She did not like the sound of that. Then again, could she trust the doctor. He had already lied to her once. He had ignored her wishes and instead given her the body that her husband had desired for her.

Already she could feel her arousal start to build. It was strange, because there was nothing about her situation that could be considered attractive or even hot. She was resting in a hospital bed, recovering from major surgery at a clinic. There was nothing sexy about it. Yet, she could feel a tingle building up between her legs. Her pussy was getting wet just laying there. Already she could feel a desire building within her to masturbate. If this continued, she would be screaming out for sex in a matter of hours, if not sooner.

Dr. Coulson was not lying. At least he was not lying about her baseline arousal. She was already finding it difficult to think. Images of her on her knees in front of a man or her bent over a table with her ass presented toward a man flashed through her mind. And each time she could feel herself grow just a little hornier. How long could she last before she started masturbating in front of the doctor.

"You're already feeling it," Dr. Coulson said. "I can tell. After years of this, I have developed an extra sense to tell when a girl is horny."

Katherine nodded her head. The grogginess and aches were dissipating, replaced with arousal. Was this what bimbos always felt? Was this why they seemed to so easily fall into the role of sex objects? Was this why they were so willing to show off their bodies and act like sluts?

"What can I do to fix this?" she finally asked.

"You'll need to go through with the memory engram replacement procedure, or MERP as I like to call it. We need to streamline your mind to make it easier for you to handle your body's new urges. You'll still be horny, but you'll be better equipped to handle it."

Katherine considered this. Her arousal continued to spike. She was already beginning to move her limbs, her body growing desperate for sexual contact. Her fingers were drifting toward her nether regions. She was already feeling a loss of control. The timeline Dr. Coulson gave her seemed too long. It was happening faster for her. She was sure of it. Katherine needed to do something. She needed relief. She could not stay like this or she really would go crazy, sooner rather than later.

"Yes," Katherine finally called out as her fingers found her clit. It was not entirely sure what she was agreeing to, given how good her fingers felt against her clit. It was a pleasure she had never felt before. It was far greater, far stronger, than any sexual pleasure she had felt in her life. Sex with Mitchell had never felt this good before. Was it just her enhanced body or was there something more at work?

"So you will go through with the MERP?" Dr. Coulson asked.

"Yes, whatever it takes," Katherine moaned as two finger found their way inside her. She arched her back as the pleasure increased.

"Then let's get you up out of that bed and into the chair," the doctor said.

Katherine managed to pull her fingers out of her pussy as the doctor helped her up. The warm blankets fell away, revealing her new body for the first time.

"Whoa," Katherine said as she caught sight of herself in a mirror. "I look younger."

"I'd peg your new age at about 38," Dr. Coulson said. "As I understand it, that drops about 7 years off your previous age."

Katherine nodded her head, seeing for the first time all that the doctor had done to her. Yes, she now sports big tits. There was no way anyone could view them as natural. They were far too big for her frame. Yet, at the same time, they looked inherently sexy. Her whole body seemed to have been worked over. She was taller, fitter, and all around sexier. But most noticeable of all was the voluminous head of blonde hair she now sported. Gone was the stringy brown hair, replaced with long golden locks. It was a gigantic improvement, making her already begin to forgive her husband for tricking her.

It only took a few moments to get Katherine situated in the chair. The doctor took his time preparing her for the procedure, attaching wired electrodes to the sides of her head. He wanted to make sure the placement was just right. Then he dropped a pair of goggles over Katherine's eyes. Her world went dark as they shut out all light. Finally he placed noise canceling earbuds in her ears. Her primary senses were now under his control. The MERP could begin.

Admittedly, when Katherine agreed to undergo the procedure, she did so only because it might give her some relief. Her mind would better be able to handle the sexual inputs of arousal that her body was now primed for. This was true, but replacing her memory engrams would mean she became a different person. She was the product of her experiences. Changing those experiences would make her a different person in many different ways.

Much of the MERP was automated by the computer. There were only a few guidelines Dr. Coulson needed to provide it. In some cases, he was given specific memories to erase or modify, but Katherine had made no such requests.

Therefore, he had free rein over her memories, allowing him to instruct the computer to do whatever he wanted. Of course, his client, Mitchell, had his own requests and Dr. Coulson fulfilled those to the letter. They had already been pre-programmed in this case, but the doctor was able to make a few small changes of his own.

When the procedure was finished, the woman sitting in the chair was no longer Katherine. She might have legally still been the same person, but the memories of her life had been altered to such a degree that she no longer considered herself to be Katherine. She was Kat. It was a simple name for a simple woman.

"Hi," Kat said cheerfully as Dr. Coulson pulled off the electrodes and removed her goggles and earbuds.

"Hello," the doctor responded with a smile. "How are you feeling?"

"I'm horny," Kat said. The filter that had once existed between her thoughts and her actions had largely been removed. She said what she thought, giving a running commentary for her now bimboish life.

"I bet you are," Dr. Coulson said. "And I bet you would like to see your husband."

Kat went starry-eyed as she imagined Mitchell. She was desperately in love with him. He was her everything. And she knew as a bimbo that she needed a man like Mitchell to control her. She was too dumb, too impulsive, to be on her own. But in exchange for protecting her from herself and the confusing world at large, she gave him her body, her mind, and her soul. It was the perfect trade.

"Uh huh," Kat finally said in agreement.

"Good," Dr. Coulson said. "Mitchell has a special plan for you. He thinks the two of you need to get married again, to renew your vows and whatnot. After all, when you two got married, you were Katherine. Now you're Kat. That requires a new wedding."

"It does?" Kat said cluelessly. She no longer remembered her past life. She was vaguely aware that she and Mitchell had been married for a long time and that they had kids, but they were only vague recollections. Most of her memories were that way. It was a byproduct of the MERP, but it also emphasized her own bimboness. If her own memories were so faulty, it helped drive home the fact she was just a dumb bimbo. It was strangely logical for a bimbo.

"It does. And I have just the outfit for you to get married in."

Dr. Coulson walked over to a small wardrobe and opened the door. Inside were several lacy white garments and a pair of high-heeled shoes. But there was no dress. Kat's new wedding would be conducted with her wearing lingerie.

Despite Katherine's unfamiliarity with some of the finer points of fashion and lingerie, Kat had no problem getting dressed. The bra and panties were a perfect match. The garter belt helped to hold up her white stockings. The shoes actually felt more natural to stand and walk in than when she was barefoot. But the final piece was the veil. That was the piece that made her ready.

"I'm ready," Kat said happily. Her mind was still recovering from the changes that had been made. New connections continued to be formed, but being guided by the doctor and then her husband, it was assured that she would continue to be the bimbo that she now was. If anything those connections would only grow stronger over time.

"I believe you are."

From the recovery room, Kat was ushered into an adjacent room that had been set up to look a little like a wedding chapel. In reality, it was a waiting room for men like Mitchell who were waiting for their wives and girlfriends to complete their procedures. Chairs had been rearranged and a small wooden arch had been brought in to create the appearance of an altar.

But the moment Kat stepped foot into the room, her eyes zeroed in on Mitchell. He was the most handsome man she had ever seen. Ten years her senior, he was wise and smart. But he was also still strong and virile. She was certain of that last part. And she needed him to be. Her body had needs and she would be relying on him to fulfill those needs.

The whole ceremony went by in the flash. She could barely pay attention to what the doctor, who acted as the wedding officiant, said as the couple renewed their vows. Kat was in no condition to read vows or even repeat after the doctor. She was lost in Mitchell's eyes. She did manage to say, "I do," when the time came, but that was it.

When the ceremony was over, Staci, who had acted as the witness, jumped up toward Kat to celebrate. It was what a bimbo would do. However, the doctor intercepted her, allowing Kat and Mitchell to kiss for the first time as husband and bimbo. Mitchell lifted the veil over her head and their lips met in a sensual kiss. It was the happiest moment of Kat's life.

The divorce was forgotten. Kat wanted nothing more than to dote on her husband, pleasing him in any way that she could. And she did not wait to start. Right there on the altar, she dropped to her knees and gracefully pulled Mitchell's hard cock from his pants. Kat wrapped her plump lips around his cock and started to suck. It had been more than ten years since she had last given a blowjob, but she showed no signs of rust. Her technique was flawless and it took little time before she was rewarded with a shot of Mitchell's hot seed spilling into her mouth. She swallowed it down greedily, loving the taste.

Afterward, Kat sat back on her haunches and looked up at

her husband lovingly. She sighed, fully content. She had done her duty. She had pleased Mitchell. And in exchange, he would keep her safe and happy. It was a perfect match.

After the wedding, Kat was required to get dressed in more appropriate clothes. As much as she would have loved to spend all day everyday wearing lingerie, that was not deemed acceptable when going out. And the pair needed to go out if they were going to go on their second honeymoon. In their first marriage, Katherine had insisted on a local trip. It lasted a couple days. Mitchell had wanted something more extravagant, but she had turned him down. This time, both husband and bimbo were in agreement. A week spent on white sandy beaches with tropical warmth was the perfect way to celebrate.

But each night, after they had returned to their villa overlooking the ocean, Kat would change out of whatever she wore that evening and back into her white lingerie. She would pretend it was their wedding night all over again, letting Mitchell fuck her in any way that he chose. She made her body fully available to him.

The first night he fucked her from behind, slapping her ass between thrusts. She had loved every second of it. The second night, he had bent her legs up until her white heels were beside her ears and fucked her that way. She had loved that just as much. The third night, he had finally decided to take her anal cherry. Kat had loved that too. Then again, it helped that anytime Mitchell fucked her, she came too. There was a new equality in their marriage that helped bond them together, closer than ever.

Katherine had never before considered the benefits of a bimbo life. But now that she was Kat, she loved every moment of being the bimbo MILF she had been turned into. There was nothing better than being her new sexy self with her big tits and tight body. But her favorite moments come late at night, after Mitchell has fucked her brains out, that she is able to snuggle up next to him in bed and let her mind go completely blank. It is in that moment that she feels total contentment, freshly fucked and completely devoid of all thoughts. Nothing else can compare.

COPYING KAT

Bernadette sat alone in the nursing home dining room. She was supposed to be joined by her daughter and granddaughter, but they canceled on her at the last minute. There was no reason given, but Bernadette knew the truth. They did not want to be with her.

The estranged family relationships were hard on Bernadette. Ever since her husband died, she had struggled to make friends. And despite still feeling she had life still to live at 80 years old, she could not find anyone, especially a man, to spend her time with.

"My, Katherine, you look amazing," came the cool voice of Eudora Edmonds. Bernadette could not help but overhear the conversation taking place at the table next to her. Eudora's family had come for a visit, just like Bernadette's was supposed to have.

The woman, Katherine, giggled at the compliment. "Call me Kat. Katherine is, like, such a boring name."

Bernadette rolled her eyes at the bimbo. One look at the woman and it was clear what she cared about. The vanity of Kat was easy to spot, what with the hair and the big tits.

Some women simply did not have the brains or the respect for themselves to make it in the world. They needed a man to take care of them. Actually, as Bernadette thought about it, she could see how it was a nice deal overall. A woman's needs were taken care of in exchange for focusing on looking good and putting out. The more Bernadette thought about it, that seemed like a grand way to spend her time. If she looked a little better herself, maybe was a little younger, she could surely score with one of the wealthier gentlemen at the home. She would at least have a friend and a love life again.

"I booked her in for a mommy makeover at B Clinic," Kat's husband said. Bernadette vaguely remembered his name was Mitchell, but she was not positive about that. She tried to ignore Eudora when she bragged about her son. "They can do more than just make people look better. They can physically reduce age. Katherine went in at 45 years old and came out being only 38."

Kat giggled again, clearly enjoying being talked about. She turned her body slightly, giving Bernadette a better view of her tits. They were quite massive. She honestly wondered how she could sit there like that without her back hurting. Bernadette had never been very big in the chest, but even she had felt a little bit of pain as her breasts began to drop with age.

However, it was the age reduction that most interested Bernadette. The idea that she could physically be made younger intrigued her. At 80, she knew her years were numbered. But it seemed a visit to this B Clinic, or whatever, could literally roll back the clock for her. How far, she did not know, but even a few years would be worth it. And it was not like Bernadette was hurting for money. Her husband had worked hard and left her with more than enough money to get by. But if she were young enough to enter the workforce again, she would have no problem getting by.

After dinner, Bernadette booted up her computer. It, like her, was getting old. It took several minutes before the computer was ready to use, much like when she woke up and started climbing out of bed. What had originally taken 30 seconds now took several minutes as she willed her decrepit muscles into action.

Bernadette's mission was to learn more about B Clinic. She wanted to know what they could do for her. Age might be just a number, but from her experience, age played a major role in her happiness. If she were even just a few years younger, there was so much more fun she could have. She would probably be able to make friends too. That would be a huge plus.

The website for B Clinic was basic. There were clinics all over the country, including one on the other side of town. That was good. She would not have to travel far. Not that she had a way to get around most of the time. Her car had been taken away from her, her daughter sighting age as the primary factor of why she should not be driving. At no point did anyone actually request to see her driving record or observe her behind the wheel. It was a hatchet job and one she still felt bitter over.

Sadly, there were no clear promises of a youthening procedure. Actually, from the website, it was difficult to explain exactly what B Clinic did. They were rather coy about the whole thing. However, knowing there was a chance, Bernadette found phone number and gave the clinic a call.

Two days later, Bernadette stepped off the bus in front of B Clinic. She had hated the idea of taking the bus, but her morning had not gone well. It started with Edith canceling on her again. No explanation was given. Just, "Hey mom, I can't take you to the clinic today." That was it. It burned her to see her own daughter treating her this way. It made her feel unwanted and ignored.

Normally, Bernadette would have called a cab, but she ended up on the bus instead, sandwiched between the guy eating an extra juicy burger on one side and a guy who made race car noises while the bus was moving. It was an unpleasant trip. But she was hopeful the trip would be worth it.

"Hi," said the bubbly receptionist behind the desk. She was all blonde hair and big boobs, brimming with excitement. "I'm Staci. You must be, um..." Staci checked the schedule on the computer. "Berna... Um, Bernadette?"

"That's me," Bernadette replied. She could not fault the woman too much. Her name was not that common anymore. It was one of the perils of old age. Some names fell out of fashion. Bernadette seemed to be one such name. There just were not that many young girls who shared her name anymore. Not that there were many to begin with. But it had fallen even more out of disuse in the past 30 years. It was another reminder of just how old she now was.

"Great, um, Dr. Coulson will be out in a minute for you. Have a seat, if you want, while you, like, wait and stuff."

Bernadette chuckled to herself as she sat down. The chairs at B Clinic were much more comfortable than the bus seat had been. However, her mind was on Staci as she pecked out something on the computer keyboard. Presumably it was some sort of notification system they used internally. Bernadette might have been old, but she was not a novice when it came to technology.

However, it was the obvious bimboness that had led to her chuckling. Watching Staci concentrate on the keyboard, already pushed out farther in front of her than should have been necessary, just so she could see over her prodigious chest, was enough to provide some entertainment.

When all this started, Bernadette was mostly interested in being young again. But the more she replayed the image of Kat in her mind, the more the bimbo lifestyle had begun to appeal to her. It had been so long since she had been with a man. It was something she missed. And Bernadette had little doubt that if she were more like a bimbo, her troubles of finding a man, or multiple men if she wanted, would be much easier. Older single men would have a hard time turning her down if she was a sexy bimbo. As long as she was happy, she could not see the harm in such drastic changes to herself.

As soon as Dr. Coulson appeared in the reception room, Bernadette was certain she was making the right choice. He appeared to be in his late 40s or early 50s and he looked every bit the doctor he claimed to be. Even before he spoke, she felt a confidence in him that she had not experienced with another doctor. And at her age, she had seen more than her fair share of doctors. Most of them had seemed useless, just wanting to run her through a battery of tests on the off chance that her aching body had a cause other than just being old.

"Bernadette," Dr. Coulson said. "It's an honor to have you seeking out our services today. If you'll follow me back to my office, we can discuss what we can do for you."

Bernadette smiled as she followed the doctor into the back. Everything was going to plan.

Once in Dr. Coulson's office, Bernadette took a seat in front of the desk while the doctor sat behind it. They both observed each other for several moments, sizing each other up.

"I'll admit, we don't often get women of your age seeking out our services," Dr. Coulson said.

"That surprises me," Bernadette countered. "I know I would do almost anything to be younger again. Then again, it doesn't sound like you do much marketing. I had a hard time figuring out all the details."

"How did you hear about us?" Dr. Coulson asked, curiosity getting the better of him.

"Her name is Kat," Bernadette answered. "She and her husband were visiting an acquaintance at my nursing home. She had changed a lot and there were questions asked. B Clinic was mentioned. They were all eating dinner at an adjacent table. I couldn't help but overhear."

"Makes sense," Dr. Coulson said as he nodded his head in understanding. "Of course, you know that we don't just make women appear younger here. Our services involve so much more."

"Yes," Bernadette said. "I want it all. I want to be a bimbo."

It was the first time she had said it out loud, but once she had, she knew it was true. She wanted this. She wanted to be like Kat. Yes, she was copying the woman, but she did not care about such appearances. She wanted to be sexy and desired. She wanted to be able to seduce men. She wanted to be young enough to actually enjoy it without hurting herself. It all depended on how far the doctor could take her.

"We can definitely help with that," Dr. Coulson said. "I should warn you, however, that with the tools at my disposal here at the clinic I can't completely reverse the aging process. I can't make you 20 again. It's possible, but it would require a trip to LA and even then, it might be difficult."

"You just take me as far as you can go," Bernadette said confidently. "I trust you."

"Do you have any other requests?" Dr. Coulson asked. He understood that his primary purpose was to reduce his patient's age, but there was so much more he could do for her.

Bernadette was not sure exactly what else she wanted. She wanted to be hot, but she did not have an idea of what that actually meant. That part of her plan had not been fully thought out. This was all about being younger again. She just assumed she would get some generic boosts to her appearance.

Her face lit up with an idea. "Why don't you focus on making me as hot as you can? I'll let you be the artist and I'll be your canvas."

Dr. Coulson smiled. "I like your thinking."

Once that was decided upon, there was only the cost of the procedure to negotiate. Not that Bernadette was in a negotiating position. She had already admitted to being willing to do anything for it. That meant she had little leverage. However, Dr. Coulson was a fair man and she was ultimately happy with the results. Edith might not be very happy that Bernadette had just spent a large portion of her inheritance, but there was no guarantee that there would be any inheritance in the end anyway. The longer Bernadette lived, the smaller the pot of money would be in the end.

"I have an opening for this afternoon if you'd like to start today," Dr. Coulson offered.

Bernadette smiled. "Let's do it."

It did not take long for the doctor to prepare Bernadette for the procedure. She actually had no idea what would happen to her. He promised she would fall asleep and when she woke up, she would have a much younger and hotter body. How he could achieve such things, she had no idea, but she was not about to argue with him if he got her the results she wanted. Soon she was on an operating table, ready to go. The anesthesia mask was placed over her nose and mouth. She breathed deeply and started to count backwards from 100. She was out cold before she reached 96.

Bernadette's eyes fluttered open slowly sometime later. Her body ached and her thoughts felt slow. She was still groggy from the drugs she had been given.

"Ugh," she complained, her voice cracking.

"Ah, good, you're awake," came the now familiar voice of Dr. Coulson. "Let me get you some water. My patients frequently are thirsty when they wake up."

Before Bernadette could look for the doctor in the darkened room, he had already slipped away to get her the water she craved. While he was gone, she took the time to evaluate her situation. There was some pain, but it was actually less than she normally experienced in her day-to-day life. That was a good sign. However, unlike the chronic pain she normally lived with, this pain felt more acute, like it would fade with time. Her body was still recovering from whatever the doctor had done to it. She could only hope that pain would disappear in a few days. Already she felt ahead of where she was.

Raising her hands up in front of her face, Bernadette began to examine the doctor's work. Instead of wrinkled and knotted hands, she found the skin to be smoother and the muscles and ligaments more flexible.

"I already love it," Bernadette said. Despite her thirstiness, she realized her voice sounded different. Her vocal cords were tighter, giving her a higher pitched sounding voice.

"I'm glad to hear it," Dr. Coulson said as he returned with a cup of water with a bendy straw sticking out of it. "I always like to hear how my work is appreciated."

Bernadette took a long drink of the offered water. It felt cool running down her throat. She could not be sure of the details, but she felt so much better than she had when Dr. Coulson put her under. The drugs were beginning to wear off and even the achy feelings were beginning to dissipate. As far as Bernadette was concerned, she had already experienced a miracle. The only question that remained was exactly how big of a miracle it was.

"Thank you," Bernadette said after parching her thirst.

Her throat felt better and for the first time she realized how her voice was softer too. She almost cooed when she talked. It had been unexpected, but it was not unwelcome.

"I bet you want to get a look at the new you," Dr. Coulson said. "I can help you to your feet."

Bernadette nodded her head. That sounded perfect. She wanted to take in her new appearance and getting a look at her reflection would be the perfect way to do it.

As the doctor helped Bernadette sit up, she felt the weight of her new breasts for the first time. She looked down to find them projecting off her chest, round and unnatural. She had assumed she would be getting an upgrade in the breast department, but these were bigger than she had anticipated. She honestly did not understand how she had failed to notice them before this moment.

"Don't judge their size yet," Dr. Coulson said at seeing his patient fixated on her new breasts. "You have to see them against the background of your whole body."

The moment Bernadette's toes hit the cold tile of the floor, she noticed how her feet did not flatten out. "My feet…"

"Will never let you stand flat-footed again," the doctor confirmed, finishing her sentence. "You're a high heels kind of woman from now on. But don't worry. Everything will make sense soon enough."

Feeling overwhelmed by it all, Bernadette simply nodded her head again. It was easier that way. Not that she had any choice. She had given the doctor complete control of her transformation. She had let him do with her what he wanted, as long as he made her as young as possible. And so far, she definitely felt younger and the parts of her that she had seen looked younger too. Although how much was still the question of the hour.

"Wow," she said as she stepped in front of the full length

mirror on one wall. It was hard to fully take in and process the fact that the woman Bernadette saw in the mirror was her. Her breasts dominated her appearance. They were so big, it would be impossible to hide them. She would forever be the woman with the big tits. Men would talk to her tits instead of her face. Women would give her disapproving looks as she walked down the street. It would be inescapable.

But none of that mattered. None of that mattered as soon as she saw her face. It was impossible to know her exact age now, but she looked better than she ever had. She had turned back her odometer to the point where she looked middle aged again. And it had been a long time since she had looked middle aged.

"How old am I?" Bernadette asked.

"Usually I'm only knocking off eight or maybe ten years. Most patients don't want anything as extreme as you requested. Although now that I see the results, I'm wondering if our marketing department needs to make a major shift in policy. Either way, I managed to take off about 40 years, I reckon."

"40 years?" Bernadette asked, disbelieving such a thing was possible. "That's, um..." She took a moment to do the math in her head. "That cuts my age in half. I can't believe it. It actually worked."

"Pretty nice, huh?"

Bernadette nodded in agreement, but her mind had already moved on to checking out the rest of her body. To begin with, she was blonde. That, by itself, was no major matter. Lots of people colored their hair. However, she had a feeling that her change in hair color was a permanent change. She would forever more be a blonde. Then again, her new hair color would fit a bimbo persona, whenever she was given that.

She would have been concerned about what came next,

knowing that Dr. Coulson would have to do something in her brain. What he needed from her was still unknown, but he would eventually need to change the way she thought. It was the only way to completely bimbofy her, which had been part of the plan from the beginning.

With her age pegged, Bernadette went back to examining her new body. It was strange, because its appearance made her feel like a stranger in her own body, but the sensations she received felt entirely normal to her. She was fully present in her body. She just did not have the same responses as she once did.

In addition to her larger breasts, softened voice, and blonde hair, Bernadette's lips went through a surprisingly growth spurt. They barely closed now, instead pouting, her tongue occasionally pushing out through the natural gap that formed. She had to focus to close her lips entirely. Additionally, her face saw a reduced nose, tighter, but also darker, skin, raised cheek bones, and larger, almost doll-like, eyes.

Beyond her face and hair, her body overall appeared sleek and toned. Her arms had newfound strength, as did her legs. She actually felt stronger than she had been at the peak of her physical fitness in her younger days. Not that physical fitness had ever been a priority for her. She had grown up wearing dresses and being soft and feminine. At least until she became a mother. Then it was the hectic life of parenthood. The fact her daughter now rejected her, made it all the worse. But that was why she had come here. She was throwing off the past and embracing a new future.

Regardless of all that, Bernadette knew one thing. She was hot now. There was no other way to put it. She was not just younger, but she was more attractive than she had ever imagined she could be. She had not just copied Kat, she had supplanted her, becoming an even hotter and sexier physical specimen. She had a feeling there would be an increase in

Viagra prescriptions at the nursing home soon enough. There were enough rich single men to keep her occupied.

Bernadette giggled as she realized what she was thinking about. She was not just thinking about being young and hot, but she was thinking about having sex with all those men who had previously ignored her. She was obviously no stranger to sex, but she had never felt such a strong desire for it before. Her pussy was practically gushing at just the thought.

"Ah, I believe you are experiencing part of the fun I added," Dr. Coulson said as he observed Bernadette's subtle actions. She squeezed her legs together and slowly gyrated her hips, all involuntarily in response to the surge of arousal she felt.

"What did you do?" She was not mad or angry. She still had no regrets. She was curious. If anything, the sudden surge of arousal felt good. She had not felt it this strongly before, but it had never been an unpleasant sensation. Only now it was dialed up to 11 and she was not sure what she could do about it.

"In my honest belief, a bimbo isn't necessarily just some random dumb slut," the doctor explained. "A bimbo is a woman who is completely preoccupied with sex. Everything she does is about looking sexier and turning people on. She appears dumb, because her sole focus is on sex and attracting sexual partners. I don't think there is a bimbo alive who could handle being a rocket scientist, but that doesn't mean they are completely stupid. They are just too focused on the important matters in life to be concerned with worldly affairs and whatnot. And as such, I have turned up your libido to the maximum. Even if I don't make any changes to your brain, you'll still end up a raging nymphomaniac by the end of the month."

Bernadette knew she was not yet complete. She expected

her mind to be altered in some fashion. After all, she had a very clear picture in her head of what a bimbo was. She now had the body. There was no doubt about that. She looked like a bimbo. However, she did not yet think like one.

"How is that any different from being a bimbo?" Bernadette asked, not seeing the difference yet.

"The process is wildly complicated, but to simplify it for you, we need to make sure you have the background knowledge to be the best bimbo you can be. Sure, it might take time, but you would eventually figure out a way to sink your long nails into a man or two, but more likely than not, you would end up as a drugged and drunk slut in a trailer park. I've seen it before. And I have higher hopes for my clients. You came here for the bimbo package and I'm going to make sure you leave here as a bimbo, not just a random slut."

Bernadette nodded her head in semi-understanding. It was becoming harder and harder to focus while her pussy spasmed. She was horny and getting hornier. There was no way she could last for much longer without doing something inappropriate, like humping the doctor's leg. He might enjoy it, but it seemed completely unprofessional. And she was not going to be a complete slave to her body. She would need to learn some semblance of control. Otherwise, she would end up in the trailer park, just as Dr. Coulson mentioned.

"Let's hurry up and do it," Bernadette said, although there was a part of her that meant have sex instead of transforming the way her mind worked. Sex sounded much more appealing, but she was not yet ready to give in to her body.

"I think you're right," Dr. Coulson said. "Let's not waste any more time on it."

The doctor led Bernadette over to a comfortable chair. He lightly restrained her, promising it was just for her safety during the memory engram replacement procedure. As he attached the electrodes to her temples, he explained how the procedure worked, how he would be rewiring her brain by recreating her past via her memory engrams. She would not just feel 40 years old, she would believe she was 40 years old, with the memories to prove it.

Of course, in the process, the doctor would add skills and experiences she would need as a bimbo, assuming Bernadette had not already learned them at some point in her life. Things like blowjobs and taking a cock up her ass would now be important skills and experiences for her. And then there were the softer skills, like how she should dress to best attract men, how she should move to make cocks hard, and how she should talk to make it clear that she really was just a bimbo through and through.

"Are you ready?" Dr. Coulson asked after he had fully set up the system. Bernadette's eyes were covered by a video capable visor. Her ears were filled with noise canceling earbuds, although neither of those things were activated yet.

"I'm ready," Bernadette said. "Make me a bimbo."

It was all the encouragement that the doctor needed. He started up the program on the computer and went to work rearranging Bernadette's mind, turning her into a bimbo, not just in body, but in mind and soul as well.

When the procedure was done, Bernadette had a dopey smile on her face. She looked like her mind had almost short circuited during sex. In fact, during the procedure, she had actually had several small orgasms. They were nothing compared to what she would feel when truly stimulated, but just the addition of certain memories had caused her body to shake in orgasmic pleasure. Dr. Coulson always loved to see that happen.

When Bernadette opened her eyes after the doctor had removed the equipment from her eyes, ears and temples, the woman inside was clearly no longer the Bernadette of old. It was obvious that there was not much going on in her head.

But that did not seem to trouble her. If anything, it made her happier. Thoughts would just get in the way. As long as she could be her sexy self, she would be fine. Certainly, a woman as sexy as her could find a man to help her if she got into trouble.

But it was more than that. Bernadette no longer viewed herself as Bernadette. She was Birdie now. Sure, she was still legally named Bernadette, but in her mind, she was Birdie, because she was flighty. As a bimbo, she was easily distracted, always having her attention pulled toward the shiny and the pretty, assuming there was not a man around to draw her attention. It was a fitting name, even if she could no longer understand why. But that was what she called herself. She was Birdie now and she found it preferable to her real name, which sounded boring and old. At 40, Birdie might not be young anymore, but she certainly was not old either. She had so much life left to live and so many men to fuck.

"I arranged an outfit for you," Dr. Coulson explained, opening a nearby wardrobe. There was underwear and a sundress hanging up. At the bottom were a pair of high heels. "You'll have plenty of shopping to do after this, but I don't think you'll mind that. I'm sure you'll have a blast."

Birdie squealed her thanks, not realizing that this had all been part of the transformation package. After all, it would not have done to send her home in her previous outfit. Not only would it not fit, it was not something Birdie would ever consider wearing. She was no senior citizen. At least she was not anymore.

"How can I ever thank you for making me such a sexy bimbo?" Birdie asked after she had put on the clothes. The thong fit her expanded ass perfectly. It was something she had not noticed before, but now it just felt like it was a part of her. She could not remember ever looking different. She had skipped the bra. It fit, but she was not in the mood to smother her girls with it. She still kept it, however, knowing it could come in handy another time. The yellow sundress had a deep scoop neck to show off her tits. And at their current size, they were definitely tits. They were big enough where a normal woman would have needed to visit a plastic surgeon several times to get up to her size. But Birdie had gotten it all in a single day. That was the kind of magic that happened at B Clinic.

Birdie could not sit still as she awaited Dr. Coulson's answer. She paced back and forth across the room, allowing her tits to bounce with each step, her heels clacking on the linoleum floor. Bernadette had given up wearing heels as she got older, realizing they were not worth it, as well as dealing with the fact they had become dangerous. A tumble could result in a broken hip. But Birdie looked completely natural as she walked around in her heels. She showed no reticence in how she moved. This was her new normal.

"Usually I accept blowjobs for a job well done," Dr. Coulson said. "However, I promised I would fuck Staci after I finished with you. She is adamant that her employment contract is properly fulfilled each month. As a horny bimbo, like yourself, she requires regular fuckings. I even wrote it into her contract, after she insisted of course. I've been so busy recently that we've fallen behind, so I am afraid Staci takes precedence."

Birdie pouted, feeling dejected. At least he had not turned her down because she was not sexy enough. But she could not compete against contractual obligations. Not that she would have been able to say either of those words without some help. Her reading skills had been severely limited, as too had her vocabulary. Her past interest in books and reading had been largely erased, replaced with interests in fashion and soap operas. It was easier for her to avoid putting much mental energy into anything.

"But I'm sure you'll find plenty of cock back at home," Dr. Coulson reasoned. "I bet there are some rich men you could cosy up to. You could even get them to write you into their will. That way when they kick the bucket, you'll be taken care of."

"Wow, Doc," Birdie said, her displeasure forgotten. "You're, like, super smart and stuff. Thanks so much."

It was the end of the workday when Birdie skipped out of B Clinic, ready to return to the nursing home. She had not figured out what she would do when the staff confronted her. The home was more of a retirement community with an assisted living center. She was too young for that, but she figured something would be figured out. She just knew that she would not be doing the figuring. That was for someone else to decide.

The bus ride back was not nearly as annoying as it had been on her way to the clinic. It was once again male heavy in terms of the riders, but there was no weirdness. Yes, everyone's eyes seemed glued to her chest, but that was only natural. She wouldn't have big tits and wear a low-cut dress if she did not want people to stare. Even the driver seemed interested in her tits. He did not even mind that she used a senior pass to get on. And he nearly rear ended a car after using the cabin mirror to continue watching her.

When Birdie was not inundated with male attention, she found herself wondering which of the men at the nursing home she should approach first. Dr. Coulson had given her a great idea to chase after the rich ones to try and get into their wills. She did not want to be a bitch about it, but she did have a lifestyle to maintain. That cost money, especially when she would probably need to find a new place to live and buy a new wardrobe. Not to mention she needed to figure out what to do about her family. But that last part could wait. She was horny and needed to find a man to fuck.

In the end, it had been a simple choice. Sherman Bosley was the man for her. He was handsome and clearly had some money stashed away. And as far as she knew, he had always been a terminal bachelor. That meant there was no family to fight with when it finally came time.

"Hi, Sherman," Birdie said as she posed in the doorway. He had just opened the door to her knock. "I was wondering if I could come in."

Sherman had always been smart. And despite the incredible changes in her appearance, he still recognized her, even if it was a vague connection.

"Bernadette?" he asked, surprised.

"Call me Birdie," she answered. "I went and got myself all bimboed up for you."

Despite Sherman's experience with women, he had not been prepared for the vision that greeted him at the door. His eyes fell right where they were supposed to, into her gaping cleavage.

"But how?" Sherman asked.

"Invite me in and I'll show you."

Despite his advanced age, Sherman could move quickly when he needed to. He pulled Birdie inside and quickly closed the door. This was turning into the best day in a long time.

As it turned out, Birdie was not much for explanations. She was much more interested in what Sherman had between his legs. And he did not disappoint. She started with a blowjob, wanting to give him a taste of what he could get from her. He was slow to get hard, but once he got there, he was big and virile. Birdie bobbed her head up and down on his shaft to the best of her ability, but even she was unprepared for the volume of cum he unloaded into her mouth.

Despite every attempt to swallow it all down, rivulets of cum leaked from the corners of her mouth and flowed down her chin, leaving speckled white dots on her exposed tits.

Normally, Sherman would have been spent after that. The skills of the newly minted MILF bimbo were too great. However, with a little medical intervention on his behalf, he was hard again in short order, ready for more.

"Sherman," Birdie said as she sat on his lap. She was painfully close to his cock, her pussy almost ready to envelope him completely. "If we're going to fuck like this, can you help me with stuff?"

"What do you need help with, Birdie?"

"I need money. I need a new place to live. I need clothes. Stuff like that."

"I'll take care of it," Sherman said with a sigh. There was no way he could say no to her. He had finally met his match, the figure that might end his bachelor days.

When Birdie finally sank down onto his shaft, she cried out in erotic ecstasy. So too did Sherman. They were both quickly climbing the stairway to orgasm, reaching a climax that they would both enjoy thoroughly. However, even as Birdie fucked Sherman, she was already thinking about what other men she could pull into her orbit. Sherman was great, but she suddenly realized that she was no longer a one cock kind of gal. She was not just a bimbo MILF, but a slut too.

Luckily there were plenty of men at the nursing home to start with. And there was definitely something about older men that got Birdie's juices flowing. Who knew, she might even start calling a few of them Daddy, assuming they were into that kind of thing.

But even as Birdie plotted her next conquests, she rode Sherman hard, giving him every ounce of energy she could give him. Her body moved, swayed, and bucked to perfect effect. And as they came together in a symphony of erotic delight, it became clear to her that it truly was better being a bimbo. Life, sex, everything. She had the perfect life and she planned to keep living it for as long as she was able. Bernadette had been given a new lease on life. As Birdie, she was going to live that life to the fullest.

SPREADING THE LOVE

Birdie loved life. As a bimbo, she never had cause for sadness or worry. And she had more men eating out of the palm of her hand than she ever could have imagined. And best of all, she was now young enough to enjoy it all.

However, no matter how much Birdie loved her new life, wining and dining with rich older men, she still felt an emptiness when she thought about her family. Her daughter and granddaughter were even more like strangers now since her transformation. There were times when Birdie thought about reaching out, but she had no idea what to say. How could she properly explain that it was better this way?

Edith, her daughter, was a proverbial stick in the mud. And she thought that before she had been turned into a carefree bimbo. Edith was just an all-around pain. She could not even hide her disdain for her mother long enough to pay her a visit. Not that Birdie was living at the nursing home anymore. She, with the help of one of her new male benefactors, had bought a house. She even had a car now too. There were perks to being young again.

Birdie was convinced Edith would be happier with her

life if she paid a visit to B Clinic. Really, she believed every woman should make the trip. Her life was so much better now that she was a bimbo. She was confident her experience would be similar for others. And once Edith was a bimbo, it would only be natural for Jennifer to join them as well. They could have three generations of bimbos then.

However, it was one night while Birdie was out with one of her benefactors for dinner that she hit on her grand idea. Sherman had left her alone at the table for a few minutes while he discussed something with the chef. Apparently they knew each other and Sherman wanted to make their night together special. Sherman was always doting on her, making sure that she was properly cared for. He loved having her on his arm when they went out. She was a beacon of beauty and proof of his virility, something she could attest to.

But sitting there alone was hard on the bimbo. She scanned the restaurant. It was still early with some of the happy hour customers still sipping their drinks. Birdie spotted a group of young men. She figured they were around Jennifer's age. They were hot. She could feel her pussy grow wet as she licked her lips. The image of her taking on two or three of them flitted through her mind. Birdie spent a lot of time thinking about sex and this moment was no different.

However, while Birdie was confident she could handle about half the group, assuming they were willing to share her, she knew her best chance at scoring a date with them was if she had a wing-woman. It would especially help if she had a wing-woman who was younger than her, a woman like Jennifer.

Birdie bit her lip as she imagined a bimbofied Jennifer taking on a group of men like that. Together they could handle them easily. Six of them to two women. Although three women would make the total odds a little better. But she knew Jennifer was the key. The group of men might not go for an older woman. At 40 years old, she was nearly old enough to be those men's mother. But throwing a little bit of younger pussy at them would surely convince them that an older and experienced woman in the mix could not be a bad thing. And the one thing that Birdie had gained since becoming a bimbo was experience. She was an expert on two things: fashion and sex. That was about all she could handle.

And as Birdie got to thinking, she realized if Jennifer joined her in bimbohood, it would be easier to then bring Edith into the fold. They would squeeze her until she gave in. Of course, that meant she needed to persuade Jennifer to join her first.

Birdie knew little about her granddaughter. They had spent little time together in recent years. And the woman that Birdie remembered from before was surely not the same woman she was today. People did a lot of growing up in college and beyond. It took time, but she would have flowered into her current self since Birdie had last been a part of her life. But there was no time like the present to right the wrongs of the past and reach out to Jennifer, hoping to arrange a meeting.

However, that would have to wait. Sherman returned and Birdie became preoccupied with looking sexy for Sherman and for the young men across the restaurant. She had caught their eyes and she decided to put on a show for them. Maybe it would help convince them to get their own bimbos someday.

It was the next day when Birdie managed to put her plan into motion. Once dinner had been finished the night before, a delicious dinner prepared specially for her and Sherman, she had been too focused on her body's growing desires to think about Jennifer. She was too caught up in her time with Sherman. He really did have a great cock. And he made sure she got full access to it. Across the whole evening, his cock had been in her mouth, her pussy, and her ass, all at various times, and sometimes more than once. Sherman was definitely her favorite play partner. He also provided her with the most financial assistance. He was her leading sugar daddy, although not her only one.

It started with a text message. Birdie, before she was a bimbo, had never sent texts. It was a technology she did not understand. But finding herself 40 years younger now, texting had become a normal part of her life. Although it was sometimes difficult to text with her long nails. They got in the way sometimes. Not that she would want her nails to be any shorter. Long nails were a part of her look. And she could always blame them for her misspellings and grammar issues, which were more a part of her being a bimbo than her nails, but it was still a valid excuse.

Birdie sent Jennifer a text message, asking if she had time to meet. She offered several possible times, wanting to make it clear that she was flexible. She wanted to make it easy for Jennifer to accept.

It turned out that maybe Birdie just needed to reach out to her granddaughter in a form Jennifer used more frequently. The immediate yes was a little surprising. Birdie has expected to have to almost beg her for a meeting.

Jennifer chose tomorrow's breakfast. That gave Birdie one day to get ready. She got the vibe that not all was well for Jennifer, though she had no idea what could be wrong. But it meant sympathy would likely be a big part of their breakfast.

Birdie took care of all the arrangements. She made a reservation at a little bistro in town. She had eaten there before with one of her sugar daddies. They had good food and it was a good atmosphere to talk. Although it would also be crowded enough where it was unlikely Jennifer would freak out upon learning about what all Birdie had done. She would look and sound remarkably different from the grandmother that Jennifer had known. She had gone from grandma to bimbo MILF in a single day. That took everyone some time to get used to. Although no one was complaining, not even the nursing home staff.

When the next day's breakfast finally arrived, Birdie made sure that she showed up a few minutes late. She had planned the whole encounter out and decided a late arrival would be best. She could join Jennifer at the table already, cutting down on the disbelief.

When Birdie stepped into the restaurant, she spotted Jennifer right away, sitting in the corner by herself. Her eyes appeared red and puffy, as if she had been crying before she arrived. There was definitely something wrong with her. The only questions were what was wrong and whether Birdie could use that to her advantage.

"Good morning, Sunshine," Birdie said as she sat down across from Jennifer, using her nickname from when she was a little girl.

"Grandma?" Jennifer said in disbelief. "Is that you?"

Birdie was thankful Jennifer had made the connection immediately. She had been afraid she would need to explain everything from the beginning and somehow convince Jennifer of her identity before the conversation could continue.

"It's me," Birdie said. "I had some cosmetic work done recently."

It was only then that Jennifer's eyes managed to travel down from Birdie's face to her big tits. Birdie had tried to dress conservatively for her meeting, wanting to leave a good impression, but there were some things she could not stand. Covering up her tits was one of them. There was always some part of them showing. If she was not showing off her cleavage, then she had managed to show off side boob. She even had a few tops designed to show off under boob, although she kept those in reserve for special occasions. This was not one of those occasions.

Birdie had worn a fitted white blouse and a black skirt to breakfast. Both would have been acceptable in both the restaurant as well as at the office, if she had a job. However, she had left more than a few buttons on the blouse unbuttoned, leaving a great deal of her cleavage on display. One more button and she would have been showing off her bra too. And her skirt was just a little too short to be properly appropriate. But with her great legs, no one was about to complain. And of course she was wearing her ever present heels. There was rarely a moment in the day when Birdie was not wearing heels of some fashion. She even had special heels she wore in the shower, all so her feet could be more comfortable.

"I'll say," Jennifer said, her face suddenly turning red in embarrassment. She would never have looked at her grandmother in that way before. "Well, um, you look great."

"Thanks, Sunshine," Birdie said with a giggle. "A lot has changed for me. I'm out of the nursing home and living on my own again. I even got a car."

"I don't understand," Jennifer said. It had been hard for her watching her grandmother get older. It was the main reason she avoided visiting. This time had been an exception, but only because of recent events in her life. She needed a familiar face. As it turned out, Birdie's face was less familiar than she had hoped it would be.

"I don't really either," Birdie said. "I met with this doctor at a special clinic and he made me younger and gave me a great body. He also, like, messed with my mind. I'm a bimbo now."

Jennifer's eyes narrowed at the mention of being a bimbo.

"What's wrong, Sunshine?" Birdie really did care about

Jennifer's wellbeing. She just had an extra interest in her, wanting her to make the leap to being a bimbo too.

"I caught Mark cheating on me," Jennifer said, nearly breaking into tears again. "He's my boyfriend. I mean, he was my boyfriend. I dumped him when I caught him with some slut at the bar. He told me he was going out with the guys, but really he is hooking up with some red-headed slut."

Birdie felt a moment of panic. She had hooked up with a guy named Mark recently. However, it was not her, what with her being a blonde now. And thinking about it, it seemed unlikely that Jennifer had been dating a guy in his fifties. She did not strike Birdie as a girl who deviated much from her age group. Although if she went bimbo, that might change.

It was at this moment the Birdie saw two paths she could follow. Both could eventually lead Jennifer toward bimbodom, but they each came with their own set of problems. She could shame Jennifer about not being pretty enough and not doing what was necessary to keep a man from straying. However, Birdie already hated to see Jennifer cry and she knew tears would start flowing afresh if she went that route. It might get Jennifer where she wanted her, but it would be painful and could potentially leave lasting damage that even Dr. Coulson could not fix.

The other option was to use this moment for revenge. She could show Jennifer the way to make herself better, better than mark, to give into her vanity and become the ultimate bimbo. It would be like a fresh start, a way to get back at Mark for cheating on her, but also make it easier to land her next man, if she wanted to limit herself to just one man. Birdie could not understand that. There were too many hot guys, there were too many rich guys, and there were too many cocks that she wanted to sample. Yes, she could have a sugar daddy for every night of the week, but she preferred to leave a few days open, giving her the chance to meet new men and have more fun.

"I'm so sorry to hear that," Birdie said. It was important to start with sympathy. She needed to prove that she was in Jennifer's corner.

"It makes me mad, because I thought we had something. I thought I was enough. But I guess I wasn't. Did you know I actually started researching boob jobs after I dumped him?"

"You have a right to be mad," Birdie said. "And if you want a boob job, I'll pay for it, if that will make you happy. I bet Mark would be upset he cheated on you if he found out you were willing to go so far as to make yourself hotter."

It might not have been the most elegant of persuasive attempts, but it was a start. It was important to get her foot in the door, to help Jennifer begin to see the advantages of not only having bigger breasts, but being a bimbo too.

"You would?" Jennifer asked, looking hopeful. "Seeing all those before and after pictures made me feel almost worse, because I know I can't afford it. I mean, I'm working and everything, but there's a car payment and I'm paying rent to Mom. It adds up."

"I just want you to be happy," Birdie said. "I even know a doctor you can talk to. He did my enhancements. I bet he could fit you in for a consultation."

"I don't know," Jennifer said, feeling the conversation was moving too fast for her. She was not ready to jump up to that level. She had been well-schooled when it came to making decisions. She knew not to make big decisions in the wake of tragedy. Catching her boyfriend cheating and dumping him was not tragic on a grand scale, but it felt tragic to a 25-year-old woman of limited experience.

"Let's eat and you can think about it."

The rest of the breakfast went swimmingly. Jennifer found Birdie's company to put a smile on her face. Yes, her grandmother now seemed a bit dim and she was far more interested in fashion and men than she had been in the past, but she seemed happy. And Birdie's happiness was infectious. By the time breakfast was over, Jennifer was smiling again.

"How about I schedule a consultation for you?" Birdie offered. "You can decide if you want to go through with it later. This is just to get you on Dr. Coulson's calendar."

Jennifer nodded her head as they exited the restaurant. "I'd like that."

"Great," Birdie said, smiling wide. "But do me a favor. Don't tell your mother about this: our breakfast and my offer. You know how she can get sometimes."

Again, Jennifer nodded. Living under the same roof as her mother made it clear that Edith could be a real stick in the mud, although Jennifer would have said Edith had a stick up her ass most of the time.

The two parted company after a hug. Jennifer still found it strange how different Birdie looked. It really was as if years had been melted away from her face. And the fact she acted younger too was really interesting. Jennifer had always believed that beauty was only skin deep, but in this case, she was wondering if that adage was wrong. The more beautiful Birdie looked, the happier she seemed to be and the better a person she had become.

Of course, there had been no mention of bimbos. Birdie had steered clear of that landmine. The negative connotations were too strong when it came to the term bimbo. Had Jennifer called the woman who Mark had cheated on her with a bimbo, she might have been lost to Birdie's cause from the start. But calling her a slut instead made it a little easier. There was room to maneuver. Now she just needed to talk to Dr. Coulson to clue him in on her plan.

Sadly, the opportunity to have Jennifer meet Dr. Coulson had to wait a few days. His practice at B Clinic was getting busier, which in the big picture was a good thing. It meant there would be more bimbos in the world. It meant bimbos were becoming more accepted and even desired. Not that Birdie could understand why bimbos experienced so much hate. They did nothing but spread joy and pleasure wherever they went.

However, Birdie used that time to her advantage. She continued communicating with Jennifer, mostly via text. She shared stories about some of the activities she got up to, although she kept things tame so as not to scare her. Most importantly, Birdie made it clear how important her big tits were to her, sharing stories about how she got free drinks and even how they helped her hook up with guys. From what she could tell, Jennifer was an enthusiastic recipient of such stories.

When the day finally arrived for Jennifer's consultation at B Clinic, Birdie had primed her for what to expect. At the same time, Birdie had also been in contact with Dr. Coulson. She wanted to make sure the whole event went smoothly and without incident. The last thing she wanted was for Jennifer to back out or get cold feet. She wanted her to be eager and fully prepared to join the ranks of the bimbofied. It was what Birdie wanted and she hoped Jennifer would come to see that being a bimbo was for the best.

"Welcome to B Clinic," Dr. Coulson said as Birdie led Jennifer into the clinic. Staci was conspicuously absent, having been sent on her lunch break so that Dr. Coulson could handle Jennifer's intake. "My name is Dr. Coulson. You must be Jennifer."

Jennifer nodded her head. This moment had felt like a long time coming, but she was also nervous. As much as she had come to enjoy her relationship with Birdie, she had to admit so much had changed. If Dr. Coulson could turn her formerly elderly grandmother into a beautiful and much younger woman, what could he do to her?

For Dr. Coulson, he smiled as soon as he saw Jennifer. Her potential was outstanding. He was certain she would make a terrific bimbo, once the process was complete. If all went well, she would be leaving the clinic a very different woman than she had entered it as. Younger and hotter was already the doctor's forte, but he had every intention to turn Jennifer into a complete bimbo. Her mind would be so severely warped and altered, she would struggle to remember her own name half the time. All she would know was that she was hot and horny and the rest would go from there.

However, Jennifer did not notice the way Dr. Coulson looked at her. He had become an expert on concealing his thoughts and real intentions. It was a necessary skill in his line of work. The women he treated always left with a smile on their faces, but there were times when they were more resistant to the idea of willfully becoming sex objects. It was in those instances that he needed to disguise his true motives the most.

It took little time before Jennifer and Birdie were seated in Dr. Coulson's office. It was Jennifer's turn to talk, describing how she would prefer to look.

"My breasts could be a little bigger. And I wouldn't mind losing a couple inches around my waist. After that, I guess blonde hair would be nice. I can't think of too much else."

"I can give you all of that," Dr. Coulson said with a knowing smirk. "And if you'd like, I'm sure I could knock a couple years off your appearance too. You must be approaching 30, right?"

"I'm 25," Jennifer shot back. "I guess a more youthful appearance would be nice. I don't want to look too young, but yeah, it would be nice to get carded anytime I try to buy alcohol. I actually miss that."

In truth, Dr. Coulson thought she looked her age. But that simple comment, making her think she looked older, was always a good way to get someone like Jennifer to jump at the chance to look younger. And it worked. The manipulation had already begun. Then again, once she had gone through the process, she would do anything the doctor said. It would be in her programming.

"I'm so sorry," Dr. Coulson said. "I just assumed. That's my fault. Anyway, if you are interested, I can fit you in this afternoon. I know this might be rushing things in your mind, but this is my only free time for more than a month. Business is really picking up now."

"Oh, wow, I wasn't expecting..." Jennifer trailed off, trying to decide what to do. She looked at Birdie, hoping to get some advice from her, but it was obvious what Birdie would say. She should go for it.

Jennifer suddenly realized how much Birdie was pushing her. She had handled all of the arrangements. She was even going to pay for everything. That was nice, but it certainly made Jennifer feel strange. She had never been one to accept much help from others. She had been raised to be as independent as possible. And until now, that upbringing had done well for her, creating an environment where she could succeed. But this was different now. Between the breakup with Mark and reconnecting with Birdie, she needed to understand that her independence might have been part of her downfall.

"I'll do it," Jennifer said.

"Fantastic," Dr. Coulson said, rubbing his hands together. "You won't regret this. You won't even know how."

And that was the truth. With most of his patients, he usually took his time between the physical and mental transformation process. With Jennifer, however, he was taking a different path. He had decided to do both as close to concurrently as possible. It was the best way to keep her unaware of the slight deviations from the plan he was taking her on. While Jennifer had expressed her desires for her modifications, it was Birdie and himself that were actually doing the choosing. Without any time for her to process her situation before the memory engram reprogramming, the easier the whole situation would be.

And from Jennifer's perspective, it was like she had fallen asleep as a plain woman and woken up as a beautiful bimbo. Although the woman whose eyes slowly fluttered open after her procedure was nowhere near the same woman as had gone to sleep in the first place.

"Birdie," she squealed at the sight of her grandmother, although now grandmother was not exactly the right description. Yes, technically it was still true, but their age differences would lead most to believe only a single generation separated them.

"It's good to see that you're awake, Jenni," Birdie said with a happy smile. She was happy to see Jenni wake up from her procedure, but also happy to see that she had turned out so well. Even just saying Birdie's name was a major clue of the radically different person Jenni was compared to Jennifer. "You're looking bimbolicious."

Jenni practically purred at that. She viewed it as a compliment. Then again, in her newly warped mind, being a bimbo was a positive. And Jenni looked and sounded like every bit the bimbo. Her hair had grown out long and blonde. It was this color permanently. She could still dye her hair, but she would not need to touch up her roots to maintain her light blonde mane. That came naturally now.

Jenni's face had been smoothed out and made to appear even younger than her 25 years. She looked 20, meaning she was actually too young for certain activities. Not that club bouncers would turn down a woman as good looking as Jenni. Her plump lips and wide eyes were enough to attract most men, especially when they took a moment to consider what her lips wrapped around their cocks would feel like.

But it was Jenni's tits that would forever mark her place in society. They were big, but not huge. Birdie was bigger. But they were just a little oversized on her frame and were a good starter set. Jenni could always go bigger later. And presumably she would want to.

But the change in Jenni's appearance was minor compared to the complete rework she had undergone in her mind. Gone were the memories of her being studious and focusing on her education. Her new memories saw her as the slut. She had learned that her best skills were physical and she had wanted to play that up ever since. If it were not for people like Birdie guiding her to be the best bimbo slut she could be, she was certain she would have gone down a deep hole, becoming a trashy slut.

There was no doubt she was a slut, however. Her libido was too high to consider any other way of life. Sex was constantly on her mind. It was not her fault that it felt so good. That was just her body's natural state.

"Mmm," Jenni purred as she ran her long-nailed hands across her tight and taut body. The memories of how she came to be this way were confusing. She knew she had just finished a major operation, but at the same time, she was aware that this was who she had always been. Such a confluence of thoughts would have left Jennifer paralyzed with self-doubt and fear. But Jenni simply ignored the contradicting aspects of what she remembered of her life. As a bimbo, she was aware that her memories were not to be trusted. Her thoughts were not to be trusted either. Unless, of course, those thoughts involved sex or looking sexy.

Those were the two things she might be considered an expert in.

"Let's get you dressed and then we can go home," Birdie said. "I've already arranged for you to move into my house."

Jenni smiled, liking the idea of spending more time with such an important role model. Birdie made a great bimbo and Jenni wanted to soak up all of her knowledge, no matter how little Birdie actually had for herself. After all, she was a bimbo too. All Jenni knew was this was the start of a wonderful adventure.

* * *

The plan was as simple as it could be. Birdie and Jenni had invited Edith to come over. It was then that they would work her over, persuade her to join them as bimbos.

Edith had already become suspicious that something was amiss. Jenni, or Jennifer as she still considered her daughter to be, had mysteriously moved out. The two of them had continued to communicate by text message, but even those messages had become off. The language Jenni used, not to mention the spelling errors, had practically transformed overnight.

However, Edith had no idea what had actually happened to her daughter. She was unaware that Jenni went out every night to hook up with guys. She had already made a return hookup with Mark, the man who she had previously dumped after she caught him cheating. She was not interested in rekindling their relationship, even as Mark was now kicking himself from straying, seeing how hot his ex-girlfriend now was. She just liked his cock. And there was the familiarity they shared with their past, even if Jenni could not specifically remember what that past was. She was just happy to have a friend with benefits relationship with him.

The shift from Jenni living at her mother's house to living with Birdie had been an abrupt change. Jenni's room at home was still full of her old clothes and belongings. The difference was Jenni no longer felt any affinity toward her past life. She was a bimbo now and there was nothing about her old life that still held sway over her. She had even quit her job, deciding it was better to balance a few sugar daddies like Birdie did. It certainly played better to her strengths as a hot slut and bimbo.

Edith would have ignored Birdie's attempts to invite her over. For whatever reason, she no longer felt a connection to her mother. It was hard to understand why. Maybe Bernadette's age was a reminder that Edith herself was in the second half of her life now. At 50, she knew she did not have too many years left. Sure, she could live for another 35 for even 40 years, but each day was one less day she had in front of her. Seeing her mother growing old was just a reminder of her own fate.

But Edith was completely unaware of what had happened. She did not know that Jenni had turned herself into a quintessential bimbo and she was equally clueless that Birdie was a bimbo milf. Nor did she realize that they were teaming up against her.

Nonetheless, Jenni inviting her Edith for a visit could not be turned down. While Edith might have avoided Birdie, she could not do that same to her own daughter. And it was for that reason that she showed up at a strange house late on a Saturday morning. And it was a good thing it was late morning. Both Edith and Jenni had only returned to the house a couple hours before, having both been out the night before with various men. They had gotten all the sleep they would need, but they had not slept at home. They probably only made it home to bed half the time they went out. The rest of the time they found other beds to sleep in.

The doorbell rang, sending both bimbos into a tizzy as they put the final touches on their plan.

"Coming," Jenni called out as she pulled her tube top up over her tits. She had been playing with them while she waited. That was one of the nice things about tube tops. Her tits were always easy to access. This particular tube top did a poor job of actually covering her. At least it did the way she wore it. The top was not long enough to cover her whole torso. Even as she left it to barely cover her nipples, it also failed to cover her belly-button. She wore a long dangling piercing there after Dr. Coulson had added it. She had several additions like that, all of which she loved. Jewelry made her feel sexy.

"How do I look?" Birdie asked as she shifted her tits in her button-up blouse. Between the two of them, Birdie looked like the responsible one and Jenni looked like the rebellious one, trying to leave as much skin exposed as possible. In addition to her tiny tube top, she also wore a pair of tie-side denim shorts that were so short they were more like underwear. Her feet were supported on a pair of wedge slides. It was a casual outfit. If she were going out, she would change into something classier.

"Like, so hot," Jenni said with a pouting smile.

Birdie had coupled her blouse with a black leather skirt with a slit up the side that showed off all of her leg. Her own feet were encased in black heeled ankle boots with a platform sole. Neither of them were wearing footwear that would allow them to move very fast.

"You should do the greeting," Birdie reminded Jenni. "That's the plan. Remember?"

"Oh yeah," Jenni said thoughtlessly. "I forgot."

Jenni shuffled over to the door and opened it wide, revealing her enhanced body to Edith and anyone on the street who happened to be walking or driving by. Ever since

Birdie had moved in, the foot traffic in front of the house had increased. Jenni's addition to the household had caused another considerable bump.

"Oh my god," Edith said, shocked at her daughter's appearance. "Jennifer, is that you?"

Jenni giggled. "Hi, Mommy. I've missed you."

"What..." It was all Edith could say. The sight of what Jenni had become both fascinated and disgusted her. But when Edith looked up to see her mother standing back a little ways, she became even more confused.

Looking from woman to woman, Edith could barely believe her eyes. They both looked younger, although Birdie had undergone the largest of changes in that regard. She looked younger than Edith did.

"Come in," Birdie said. "We need to talk and stuff."

Before Edith could even begin to think about how this had happened to the two other women in her family, she found herself stepping into the house. Jenni stepped aside and guided her mother deeper into the house, toward the living room.

"What happened to you, Sunshine?" Edith finally managed to ask. They were the only words that seemed to make it through the confusion in her mind.

"I visited a special place and they gave me this hot body and made me feel, like, totally happy and sexy."

Edith blinked, saying nothing. That was not the answer she had expected. Not that she had expected a specific answer. But she had thought she would get more than that. Everything about Jenni seemed different. She could not believe her daughter would just move out of the house like she had. Nor could she believe that her daughter had gone off and gotten implants and dyed her hair. And then there was how she was dressed and spoke. Jennifer never would have dressed like this before and her voice sounded different, like she was one of those valley girls from LA. None of it made any sense.

Jenni guided Edith to the couch where they both sat down. Birdie sat down across from them in an armchair. She had to make sure to keep her knees together. She was not wearing any panties.

"What's going on?" Edith asked. "What do you want? Mom, what have you done?"

"Call me Birdie," came her answer. "Everyone does now. And it's not like I look like your mom anymore. We could be sisters."

"You'd be the hotter sister," Edith said automatically.

Birdie shrugged her shoulders. "It doesn't have to, like, be like that. That's why we, um, called you here and stuff."

"What the hell happened to you?" Edith pressed, her voice a mixture of fear and anger. She was angry, because Jennifer had ruined her life, seemingly at the hands of her own mother. And she was afraid, because she felt like the walls were pressing in on her.

"I got turned into a bimbo," Birdie said. "And it's great. I love it. And I wanted to, um, share it with both of you."

"Jennifer, why?"

"Call me Jenni," she answered with a giggle. "I was, like, mad and unhappy, 'cause, like, I broke up with Mark and it was sad. But then Birdie showed me how cool it is to be a bimbo. I don't remember lots of stuff now, but it's okay, 'cause guys are so much smarter than me."

"Don't say that," Edith said, appalled by her daughter's admission that she was dumb.

Jenni shrugged. "It's okay. It's, like, totally better being an airhead. No more stupid thoughts to get in the way and stuff. I get to be super hot and super horny and life is amazing."

"What do you want from me?" Edith asked, turning her attention back to Birdie. "Are you just torturing me?"

Birdie shook her head no. "We want you to join us."

"Never," Edith cried out defiantly. "I won't. You can't make me."

"Why are you being all mean and stuff?" Jenni asked, pressing her body into Edith's side. It was a closeness that Edith remembered, back when it had been her job to comfort Jennifer. But it was different now. Jenni was all grown up and apparently had given up her promising life as a smart and independent woman to become a submissive bimbo.

"I'm not being mean," Edith tried to counter. However, it was impossible to change Jenni's mind of that.

"We just want what's best for you," Birdie said.

It did not help that Birdie sounded so calm and wise, despite the radical changes she had undergone as well. She did not even sound the same. Her voice was soft and higher pitched than Edith could remember. It was becoming increasingly apparent that Edith was now the odd woman out in the family.

And the truth was, she missed her family. Edith felt the weight on her shoulders every time she had ignored Bernadette's phone calls or made up an excuse as to why she could not visit. At the time, she had at least been able to spend time with Jennifer. But now she felt like both of them had disappeared from her life, both of them were against her. It was not a pleasant position to be in, to feel like she had lost her family.

"Jenni, are you still working?" Edith asked, suddenly concerned about her daughter's welfare.

"Nuh uh," Jenni said, shaking her head. "Jobs are silly."

"But how will you get enough money to eat and live?"

"That's what boys are for," Jenni answered with a giggle.

Edith looked up toward Birdie, hoping she might be able to talk some sense into her.

"I taught her that," Birdie volunteered. "Sexy women like

us don't work. We just have fun. We let the guys deal with the hard stuff."

"Gah," Edith practically screamed. "What about being strong independent women? Aren't you ashamed of the example you're setting for Jenni here. You're teaching her to be submissive and let men run her life."

"It's okay, Mommy," Jenni said soothingly. "You're just a girl like us. You don't have to know those answers. It's just easier this way."

"More fun too," Birdie added as she got up and moved to the couch, sitting on the other side of Edith from Jenni. "It was so hard before, when I was old and boring. You wouldn't visit me. None of the men would talk to me. I was lonely. But now I'm younger and hotter and everyone wants to be my friend. And those men who are my friends now like to buy me stuff. They bought me this house and my car. Why shouldn't I let them take care of me when I do such a good job of taking care of them?"

"But…" Edith said, but her protest died on her lips. It was getting harder and harder to hold out against the overwhelming presence of Birdie and Jenni. And it was not as if Edith had never dreamed about being sexy and playing dumb for men. She had even tried it a few times, but she had always failed. But there was no way she could fail if she were younger and hotter and maybe a little dumb for real. It would be easy then. It would be fun.

"No," Edith cried out as she shook off Birdie and Jenni and stood up. She started to pace around the room, trying to organize her thoughts. "I can't stop either of you from being bimbos, but I won't do it."

"But, Mommy," Jenni whined.

"That's all right, Sunshine," Birdie said, cutting off Jenni's petulance. "Your mother doesn't, like, need to join us. She can totally be a loner. No friends. No family. I was like that. It made me sad. But will never, like, feel that way again."

"Because you're a bimbo?" Jenni asked.

"Because I'm a bimbo," Birdie agreed. "Now go upstairs and get changed. We're going out."

Jenni jumped up and scurried upstairs to her room to get changed. She loved to go out, whether it was to go shopping or to go to clubs and parties. It was all fun for her.

Edith stopped her pacing and watched as Birdie and Jenni leapt into action. It was hard to deny that Jenni seemed happy with her life this way. Not that seeing her turn herself into a willing sex object for men was easy for her. But there was no doubt that Jenni was a sex object. Her breasts, her drool-worthy body, her long blonde hair. Everything about her screamed sex.

Edith shuddered at the thought of what Jenni got up to on her nights out. She was an adult, but it was still difficult for her, as a parent, to admit that Jenni was fully grown and making adult decisions.

It was difficult to accept the changes to Birdie as well. Edith felt like she was the oldest in the family now. And she looked it too. Edith caught sight of her reflection in a mirror. The bags under her eyes, the wrinkles around her mouth. Her skin appeared sallow. It was stress related. But that did not stop the fact that Edith did not feel good about herself. The comparison between her and the rest of her family was striking.

As much as Edith disliked the idea of giving up her independence, she had to admit there were some benefits to being younger and hotter. There were benefits to not being caught up in the world at large. There were benefits to not worrying and letting others take on the hard work for a change. And there were benefits to being so sexy. She was sure the sex was amazing. Edith had not had sex in a long time, as least not with another man. The only thing that had been between her legs in recent years ran on batteries.

Considering how long Edith expected Birdie and Jenni to get ready for their day out, she was surprised to see Jenni back downstairs so soon. Then again, Jenni had not needed to change her clothes that much. The tube top and shorts had been replaced with a pink wrap dress that actually looked surprisingly normal on Jenni's figure. She still looked amazing in it, with her tits on perfect display. And it was short enough where Edith guessed it would not be difficult for anyone who wanted to find out if she was wearing panties or not. Edith's best guess was no, since that just seemed to be how Birdie and Jenni rolled. Panties would just get in the way of their extracurricular activities, which seemed to be their primary focus in life now.

Interestingly, Jenni had added a black collar with her name spelled out in rhinestones. It looked good on her, but Edith could not help but feel it was another way in which she had lost her daughter. She was used to Jennifer, but she was Jenni now. She was a bimbo through and through.

It only took another minute or so for Birdie to appear at the top of the stairs. She had replaced her outfit with a sleeveless pink sweater dress. The dress appeared more conservative at first, but as Birdie turned slightly, Edith could see it was anything but conservative. The part of the dress that covered her chest was too narrow, leaving significant side boob on display. There was little risk of a wardrobe malfunction, but it was still a significant shock for Edith.

Birdie, like Jenni, was wearing a collar with her name spelled out in rhinestones. Once again, it was a reminder of how Edith did not belong. It set her apart from the two remaining members of her family. *I made her an outsider.*

It was at that moment that Edith understood her situation. It was at that moment that the problem before her came into focus. This was less about the sexy body and the bimbofied brain. It was about her relationship with the only two women in her life. She had a choice to make, but in some ways it was no choice at all. Her decision had been made as soon as Jennifer had agreed to become Jenni.

"I'm in," Edith suddenly said. "I'll be a bimbo."

"Yay," Birdie and Jenni cheered. They rushed Edith and wrapped her up into a big hug. It was hard not to smile. Their happiness was infectious. Edith could not believe what she had just agreed to do, but she felt oddly at peace with the situation. Whatever happened, she was reuniting with her family. It just so happened that her family were bimbos and she would soon join them in that regard.

Despite the fact it was a Saturday, the trio showed up at B Clinic without an appointment. Dr. Coulson was there, as was Staci.

"I didn't expect to see either of you again so soon," Dr. Coulson said. "I wasn't expecting anyone today."

Birdie and Jenni smiled at the sight before them. Edith, however, recoiled at seeing Staci's blonde head bobbing up and down in Dr. Coulson's lap. If she heard the visitors, she did not seem to care that she now had spectators. For Staci, completing her blowjob was far more important than her role as a receptionist.

"Maybe we should come back another time," Edith said as she shifted back toward the door. She was beginning to have second thoughts about everything. Could she really go through with an operation that would turn her into a bimbo? It seemed preposterous, but knowing what had happened to Birdie and Jenni made it all too real.

"It's fine," Dr. Coulson said calmly. He did not seem embarrassed by being caught in the act either. "Staci here is almost done. Then we can go back to my office and discuss your treatment options."

Edith found herself nodding her head in agreement. That sounded like a good idea. It was only as Dr. Coulson came in Staci's mouth that Edith noticed Jenni and Birdie were holding her arms, keeping her from escaping. Not that she was trying to leave, but she figured it would be difficult to fight them off if she suddenly decided to leave. Had they been their old selves, Edith knew her mother would have been no trouble. It would have come down to Jennifer and Edith was confident she could handle her daughter in that regard. But that was before they had been bimbofied. There was no telling what hidden strengths they now possessed.

A moment later Dr. Coulson was zipping himself up and rising from the receptionists chair. Staci licked her lips as she replaced him, taking her normal position. "Thank you for waiting. I wasn't expecting anyone else today so I figured I would give Staci a bonus."

Staci smiled vapidly. She seemed only vaguely aware of the situation. However, Dr. Coulson was taking charge and he was already beckoning Edith and her bimbo companions toward his office.

"You must be Edith," Dr. Coulson said once they had gotten settled in his office. "Birdie has told me so much about you. She knew you would be a hard nut to crack, so that's why we dealt with Jenni here first."

At hearing their names, both Birdie and Jenni sat up a little straighter, pushing their already prodigious chests out. It was an automatic response.

"Your little plan worked," Edith said. "Here I am."

"Actually, it was Birdie's idea," Dr. Coulson said. "She arranged for all of this. And she's paying for it too. But the only question is what to do with you. I assume you are ready to join them as a bimbo. To be honest, I was thinking you should split the difference with them. Birdie is 40 and a total MILF. Jenni is 20 and is into older men. We could make you

30 and pump up your tits so you're somewhere between them. If Jenni has had one boob job and Birdie is on her third, going bigger each time, That would put you on your second. I think that sounds about right. There's a sort of symmetry in this, I think."

Edith found herself nodding her head. That sounded about right.

"But what about my mind?" Edith asked. "You did something to their brains, I know. But what do you have in mind for me?"

"You're actually asking a worthwhile question," Dr. Coulson said. "Your two companions were not so inquisitive. They were more focused on the outcome. But I don't have a problem sharing what I'll be doing to you. Admittedly, you won't remember how any of it works once it has been completed. You see, I have equipment that reads memory engrams, those that the physical manifestations of your memories. For you, I would be deleting some of those memory engrams and reprogramming others. By the time you leave here, you will not only love being a bimbo, but you won't be able to fully recall being anything other than a bimbo. The success rate is off the charts. In all my time using it, I have never had an issue. That means no complications and no counter indications. It's full proof."

Edith swallowed hard, realizing that her time as herself was quickly coming to an end. Once she agreed to the procedure, she would no longer be Edith. She would be a bimbo instead. It was not something she was fully prepared for. Then again, how could she prepare herself for such a thing. Before today, she did not even think it was possible. Yet here she was, sitting beside her bimbofied family, talking to the doctor who had performed the procedures that had turned them into bimbos. Now it was her turn.

"When can we start?" Edith asked.

The doctor smiled. "Right away."

* * *

Waking up after the procedure, Edie felt as if she were in a dream. Her body felt divine, the way every sensation seemed to turn her on. Then again, she had some help in that regard.

The full list of alterations and changes made to her body was long. But what mattered most was that Edie loved it all. She loved her younger appearance. She looked 20 years younger and she felt it too. The wrinkles were gone. So too was the aching back and the jolts of pain she had sometimes felt in her knees.

But those changes felt minor compared to her large tits. Each one was capped with a perky nipple. The reason for the perkiness was two-fold. One, she was horny. She was always horny, but that was another matter. And two, her nipples had been pierced, keeping them erect at all times. The piercings had been a surprise. She had not expected them, but they made her unique, at least as far as the other two bimbos she knew.

Edie also had another important piercing of note. Her clit hood had been pierced vertically, leaving a piece of jewelry to always rest against her clit. Just moving around was enough to stimulate her. It was a constant reminder that she was a sexual object. And there was little doubt that Edie was as close to a sexual object as a real woman could become. Her mind had been emptied of all those useless facts and figures she had collected in the working world. Her mind had been severely altered, leaving her unable to do more than extremely basic reading and counting on her fingers.

But what Edie lacked in intelligence, she more than made up for in enthusiasm and sexual desire. Every movement was made with sex in mind. And even looking around the room,

Edie noted how each piece of furniture could be used in the act of sex. For Edie, fucking was like an art form and she was an artist. Nothing else really mattered beyond that. Everything else she did was with the purpose of passing the time between fucking or part of the act of attracting a man to fuck her.

It felt as if a whole new world had been opened up for her. Edie was vaguely aware that she had not always been like this. But now it was all she could think about. Sex was constantly on her mind. Even seeing Dr. Coulson left her wondering how big his cock really was. She had caught a brief image of it when she had first arrived, but that was when she was Edith. Her life as Edith was now a distant memory. In Edith's place was Edie, a slut and a bimbo.

It was amazing that Dr. Coulson had managed to complete his work in a single afternoon. To think he could alter a woman's body and mind, turning her into a quintessential bimbo over the course of a couple hours was truly impressive. Then again, with the back of the Bimbo Ward, he had access to medical technologies that were still a pipe dream for the rest of the world. Bimbofication research was not exactly something that leant itself to the mainstream. The world at large was not yet ready for all that the Bimbo Ward and the related B Clinics could do. The services they provided were still kept a secret even as each new bimbo created increased the risk of gaining attention.

But Edie cared about none of that. She could not even comprehend all the technology and medical knowhow that had gone into her transformation. She was far more interested in rewarding Dr. Coulson for his fine work. However, it seemed that was not on the menu for the newly minted bimbo. Waking up, she was greeted with her bimbo family. Birdie and Jenni looked down on her with broad smiles.

"You're hot," Jenni said, speaking her mind without a filter. "I'm so, like, happy you chose to be a bimbo and stuff."

"Come on, baby," Birdie said, pulling the blanket off Edie's prone form. "Let's get you dressed so we can go party."

At the mention of a party, Edie jumped out of bed excitedly. She was ready to walk out the door, ignoring the fact she was completely naked. Not that nudity mattered to her. Edie was perfectly comfortable in her birthday suit. However, the rest of the world was not so comfortable with that.

"We brought you some clothes to wear," Jenni said.

"And we bought you a collar to match ours," Birdie added.

"Oh goodie," Edie said as she spotted the pile of clothes on a nearby chair. There was a pink body con dress with a large keyhole cutout over her tits. It meant even without a low neckline, she would still be able to show off her tits. That was now of paramount importance. The dress was tight, hugging her curves with delicious results, keeping tight around her narrow waist, but with enough room to fit her tits and the flare of her hips.

The collar and strappy high-heeled sandals rounded out the look. No one would ever have guessed Edie had once been a conservative middle-aged woman. She looked every bit the blonde bimbo party girl that she now was.

It did not take long for Edie to adapt to her new body and her new outfit. By the time the trio reached Birdie's car, Edie moved as gracefully as her two companions. Each movement was performed with the single purpose of turning others on. It was not even a conscious decision. It was now innate. It was instinct. Edie had become a sexual being and every part of her life now reflected that, from the way she moved, to the way she talked. Life was a constant state of seduction.

"Um, like, where are we going?" Edie asked. As the middle bimbo of the trio, she was given the prospect of sitting in the passenger seat. Birdie was behind the wheel and Jenni sat in the back seat. She was the youngest, after all.

"There's, like, this cool house party tonight," Jenni answered, leaning forward between the seats, pressing her tits into the shoulders of Birdie and Edie. "I bet there's gonna be, like, lots of hot guys there."

That sounded good to Edie. She was horny and could use a hot stud to fuck her. Then again, that was her new baseline. She would always be wet and ready for sex. Her body and mind had been built for it. And if anything, she was probably the biggest slut of the trio, which was impressive given the other two's proclivities.

It was hard to separate their bimbo natures from their slutty behaviors and desires, however, there was a difference. The bimbo side of them kept them focused on what they were best at. It helped narrow their focus, making them otherwise seem dumb, even if they were brilliant at the few interests they had. Looking pretty and sexy topped their list, making them seem dull and dim witted in most standard contexts. Adding the sky-high libidos they each had, it was little wonder that they had turned into sluts as well. Not that anyone was complaining. They enjoyed it, as did the men they regularly met up with. As far as the bimbos were concerned, it was a win-win situation, even if they did not have the interest in such philosophical ideas.

The party was already rocking when Birdie pulled the car up to the curb. The three bimbos poured themselves out of the car, being careful not to completely give away the goods before they even got started. Whistles sounded out from the gathering on the front porch, the smokers who needed a break from the party inside.

The three bimbos, led by Birdie, sashayed and minced their way up the front walk. Climbing the steps, they emphasized the bounce of their tits, making sure every eye was on them. Once inside, they made a bee-line toward the kitchen where a bevy of various alcohols had been put out. Despite Jenni being underage, she played the role of bartender, pouring three drinks from the various bottles.

"To being bimbos," Birdie said in toast once Jenni had handed out the drinks.

"To being bimbos," Jenni and Edie repeated in unison, tapping their plastic cups together and then chugging down the contents. The alcohol burned on the way down, but none of them minded. They did not even need alcohol to get into the mood, but they knew a little inebriation was sexy. It was all about getting into the partying mood.

As bimbos, their alcohol tolerance was limited. As such, it took little time for them to begin to feel its effects. That, however, did not stop them from hitting the dance floor, which happened to be the living room, which had been cleared of furniture, giving space for the partiers to dance and enjoy themselves.

It did not take long before the three bimbos were approached by groups of men, hoping to get with the three hottest women at the party. No one seemed to mind that Birdie and Edie looked older than the average party-goer. They were too hot for anyone to care.

The first few men to approach them got brushed off. Just a smile and a giggle was enough to send them on their way. But then three men approached. They were each hot in their own way, each of them sporting plenty of muscles. This time, the bimbos nodded their agreement and soon they had paired off with the men, grinding more than dancing, enjoying the public foreplay.

One by one, each of the bimbos was eventually led upstairs and away from the party. The three men happened to be the three party hosts.

Birdie ended up riding her stud to a series of delicious

orgasms. Her man was enamored with her big tits, sucking on her nipples and motor boating them half the time.

Jenni just flipped up her dress and let her man take her from behind. Her eyes rolled up into the back of her head as she got pounded, enjoying every moment of it.

For Edie, the process leading to sex took a little longer. It was not because she was not eager. Edie wanted nothing more than to get filled with cock. However, the man she had paired up with was taking it all a little slower.

"Show me those tits of yours," he commanded.

Edie was pulling her dress down to reveal her fresh pair of tits to the young man before she even mentally registered the command. Her body acted of its own accord, ignoring the signals from her higher brain functions.

"Do you like my big tits?" Edie asked. "I just got them."

"They look great," the man answered. "I especially like the jewelry."

"Me too," Edie cooed. "They always make my nipples pop. And pink is my favorite color, 'cause I'm, um, a bimbo."

The man laughed. "Yes, you are. You're the hottest bimbo I've ever seen."

"But that's not the only jewelry I have," Edie continued. "Would you like to see what else I have pierced?"

"Definitely."

With her dress already hanging around her torso, Edie shimmied out of it, pushing it down over her hips until it slid down her legs. She stepped out of it and then spread her legs to give her partner for the night a better view.

"It helps keep me horny," Edie explained.

"I bet. Now let's see if I can help you with your horniness problem."

Being horny was not a problem for Edie, but she was not about to say anything. And even if she had been about to say anything, her partner dropping his pants was enough to silence her. She could only stare in awe as the biggest cock she had ever seen was displayed before her. It was hard and throbbing already, her body doing its job in turning him on.

The man guided Edie back to the bed and laid her down. A moment later he had joined her, straddling her voluptuous body, his cock primed and ready at her entrance.

"I'm going to fuck you now," the man said. "I'm going to be rough and fuck you hard. Got it?"

Edie bit her lip and nodded her head. She felt lightheaded from her arousal. But she could not imagine any place she would rather be or anything she would rather be doing. This moment was perfect. It was perfect because she was a slutty bimbo who was about to get the best fucking of her short bimbo life. Nothing else mattered.

The moment the cock pushed into her pussy, Edie squealed with excitement. It felt so good. It felt better than good. She already felt as if she was on the edge of cumming and this was just the beginning.

As she was already so wet, her partner had little issue with developing his rhythm. He started slow, easing into it, but he accelerated with significant force. Within a minute, he was fucking Edie hard, driving the air from her lungs with every thrust. His hands grabbed her tits to help keep her steady, but that only served to set off fireworks in her brain. She was cumming and still he fucked her.

"Yes," Edie managed to hiss as her lungs were emptied of air with another brutal thrust. It was all she could say, all she could do. She had been turned into a rag doll with a single purpose. She was a breathing sex doll.

The man had impressive stamina as he continued to pound into her, over and over again. Edie was in heaven. She could already feel another orgasm approach after having barely recovered from her first. The continued fucking made it all the better, limiting the post-orgasmic drop, pushing her right back up toward another climax, this time building even higher.

And then it happened. With her partner's incredible pace, it was little wonder he had managed to last as long as he already had. His cock twitched inside of her, signaling that he had reached his point of no return. He was going to cum. The only question was when and where.

"I'm gonna cum," the man roared.

"Do it," Edie managed to say, egging him on. "Cum in my pussy. Fill up my MILF pussy."

And that was exactly what he did. He buried himself inside of her as his cock began to surge with his hot white seed. Edie was cumming too. Her pussy spasmed around his cock, her body filling with wave after wave of orgasmic pleasure. Her eyes rolled up into the back of her head as her vision turned white. It was the single greatest moment she had ever experienced, already making her previous orgasm seem minor.

Edie was still breathing heavily when her partner for the evening dropped onto the bed beside her. His energy seemed spent, but as she glanced toward his cock, she saw that it still had the promise of more. Without even thinking about it, she sat up and slipped off the bed, kneeling between her partner's legs. Moments later, her plump lips were wrapped around his cock, urging it back to hardness.

There was no definite plan for Edie. Her mind was moving slowly, already rocked by two orgasms. She was operating on autopilot, doing what seemed natural in the moment. And at that moment, her instincts told her to suck cock.

It was only later that Edie realized she had never gotten her partner's name. She shrugged it off, realizing it did not matter. Names were unimportant where cocks were involved. Sure, if he was someone who was going to become a regular part of her sex life, there would have been reason to learn his name. However, he was just a passing experience, a man to pop her bimbo cherry, nothing more. It would only be later, once she had settled into her new bimbo life, that she would start to hunt for sugar daddies to take care of her. There was no way she was going back to her job. She was a bimbo now and she had other priorities.

It had been a busy few days for Jenni and Edie. On short notice, they had shed their former lives and become bimbos. Jenni was the baby bimbo in the family, the youngster who had a long bimbofied life ahead of her. Edie, on the other hand, was already in a position to call herself a MILF. And she technically was a mother, although many of those memories were now absent from her mind. Nonetheless, it was a role she was going to relish, fucking young studs and rich older men alike.

Luckily, both Jenni and Edie had a fantastic role model in Birdie. She could mother them, showing them the ropes on how to be their best bimbo selves. And together, they would prove that it really was better being bimbo.

ABOUT THE AUTHOR

Sadie Thatcher is a longtime author of erotic fiction, especially related to transformations and bimbofication. She likes to say "I have thrown off the shackles of my conservative upbringing and now write erotic stories."

She maintains several blogs devoted to her writings, including a behind the scenes look at her writing process, and bimbos in general, as well as highlights works by other authors. They can be found at:

https://authorsadiethatcher.tumblr.com
https://buildingbettergiggles.tumblr.com

ALSO BY SADIE THATCHER

Tales from the Bimbo Ward: Tegan
Tales from the Bimbo Ward: Susan
Tales from the Bimbo Ward: Joy
Tales from the Bimbo Ward: Katherine
Tales from the Bimbo Ward: Sarah
Tales from the Bimbo Ward: Salt and Pepper
Tales from the Bimbo Ward: Amanda
Tales from the Bimbo Ward: The Staff
Mistaken Identity
My New Bimbo Life
Keep Calm and Be a Good Bimbo
(Virtual) Reality
Side Effects
Plaything of Olympus
Experiment in Submission
Bimbo Bet
Snow White and the Evil Witch
Twelve Days of Bimbo
Chosen
The Faerie's Gift
The Bimbo in Yellow
Bad Role Model
Truth or Bimbo
Truth or Bimbo College Edition

Bimbo Dome

Acting the Part

Subliminal Society

Inheritance

Company Morale

His Bimbo Girlfriend

The Bimbo Room

The Bimbos of Blossom

Dr. Jekyll and Missy Hyde

Second Chance

From M&As To T&A

Trading Places

The Bimbo Nutcracker Suite

Milked and Herded

Fitting In

Clowning Around

Transformative Ink

Choices

Rival Competition

Alien Womanhood

The Curse of Playing Bimbo Tag

The Curse of Playing Bimbo Tag: Jenna or Jenni

The Bimbo Professor: The Curse of Playing Bimbo Tag Book 3

Anything for the Job

Anything for the Job 2

Anything for His Job

The Bimbo in the Mirror

The Bimbo in the Mirror 2

Astrid and the Bimbo Bee

Bella and the Bimbo Bee

Cali and the Bimbo Bee

Desiree and the Bimbo Bee

Ember and the Bimbo Bee

Fiona and the Bimbo Bee

The Intern

The Lawyer

The Hacker

Cause & Effect

Witless Protection

Stealing Sally

Simple and Fun Volume 1

Simple and Fun Volume 2

Simple and Fun Volume 3

Bimbo Halloween

Bimbo Christmas

Bimbo Technology

Dorm Room Bimbo

Carissa's Magic Pen

Spirit Walk

Muscle Memory

The Case of the Bimbo Wife

Changes

Changes 2

New Year New You

The Bimbo Dream

The Wedding Gift

The Cure

Backfire

Bim & Bo Yoga

Wishing for Each Other

Bimbo Roots

A Bimbo at Oktoberfest

The Lost Bet

The Fountain

Bimbo Ghost

Sugar and Spice and Everything Nice

Basic Bimbo

A Helping Hand

Bimbos in Space

Christmas Train to Bimboton

Letters to Bimbo Claus

Gone Fishing

The Bimbo Behind the Mask

Be Hot, Not Smart

Rival Wishes

What's in a Name?

Playing the Game

Friendly Wishes

My Chemical Bimbo

To Be Young Again

Body Swap Rings: Happy Anniversary

Body Swap Rings 2: Wedding Night

The Bimbo Experience

The Bimbo Experience 2

The Bimbo Experience 3some
The 4th Bimbo Experience
Bimbo Genes
Bimbo Genes II: The Virus
The Bimbo Genes III: The Epidemic
Bimbo Juice: Blue Raspberry
Bimbo Juice: Grape
Bimbo Juice: Mango
Bimbo Juice: Pineapple
Bimbo Juice: Red Apple
Bimbo Juice: Veggie
Bimbo Juice Gone Wild: The Muse
Bimbo Juice Gone Wild: Street Racer
Bimbo Juice Gone Wild: Score
Bimbos of the Traveling Earrings: Book 1
Bimbos of the Traveling Earrings: Book 2
Bimbos of the Traveling Earrings: Book 3
Bimbos of the Traveling Earrings: Book 4
Bimbo Party: Kennedy
Bimbo Party: Esme
Bimbo Party: Ariana
Bimbo Party: Tara
Workout Buddies
Wishful Thinking
Wanting More
Bimbo Harem: Annabelle
Bimbo Harem: Josie
Bimbo Harem: Nikki

Bimbo Harem: Tiana
Giggle Dust
Giggle Dust 2.0
Giggle Dust 3.0
Giggle Dust 4.0
Bimbo Takeover: The First Step
Bimbo Takeover: Teammates
Bimbo Takeover: Going to the Top
Bimbo Takeover: Revenge of the Bimbos
Discovering Eden

Printed in the USA
CPSIA information can be obtained
at www.ICGtesting.com
LVHW021622061224
798539LV00032BA/608